I0730996

Praise for Peter N. Dudar's
Blood Cult of the Booby Farmers!

"…disgustingly violent, it contains
scenes of disgusting sex, and…disgusting
characters…depraved…
a masterpiece of extreme fiction."
–TT Zuma, Horror World

"…reads like an exploitation film showing in Times
Square in its heyday…obscenely dark…"
–Colleen Wanglund, Monster Librarian

Also by Peter N. Dudar

The Goat Parade

BLOOD CULT OF THE
BOOBY FARMERS

PETER N. DUDAR

A
Grinning Skull Press
Publication
PO Box 67, Bridgewater, MA 02324

Blood Cult of the Booby Farmers
Copyright © 2022 Peter N. Dudar

All rights reserved. No part of this book may be used or reproduced in any manner whatsoever without written permission except in the case of brief quotations embodied in critical articles or reviews.

This book is a work of fiction. All characters depicted in this book are fictitious, and any resemblance to real persons — living or dead — is purely coincidental.

The Skull logo with stylized lettering was created for Grinning Skull Press by Dan Moran, http://dan-moran-art.com/.
Interior graphic designed by Alexey Berezov.
Cover designed by Jeffrey Kosh, http://jeffreykosh.wix.com/jeffreykoshgraphics.

All rights reserved.

ISBN-13: 978-1-947227-73-6 (paperback)
ISBN: 978-1-947227-74-3 (e-book)

DEDICATION

For my mother, Christie Marie Dudar, with all my love.

Thank you for everything.

Please don't read this!

ACKNOWLEDGMENTS

Stop! This is my opportunity to give you, the reader, fair warning. At the heart of this novella is a woman-survivor story, and it depicts graphic scenes of violence and sexual assault. It was originally written and published as an homage to the exploitation books and movies of the late 70s and early 80s. I'd like to thank my friends at Grinning Skull Press for helping me return my story to the world of print and for their excellent edits and suggestions, which made an enormous difference in my storytelling. Special thanks to Jeffrey Kosh for creating the cover art that absolutely captured the essence of exploitation cinema movie posters. Love and thanks to Nick Cato, who originally published my book in 2013. And my undying gratitude to those who've already read my book and offered support and positive reviews. You guys rock!

CHAPTER 1

Mathias wasn't quite retarded, but he *was* fifty shades of inbred. And with the conjoined head of his deformed twin brother lurking beneath the bib of his overalls ("the talking lump" he called Bubba), the boy was nothing more than a freak that spent his days arguing with himself. Papa often thought about taking the boy out behind the barn, putting the barrel of his shotgun up to his head, and pulling the trigger, but farm life was hard and he needed the extra pair of hands to harvest crops and bail hay and do chores around the Tucker homestead.

And it wasn't like the boy didn't pull his weight.

Mathias was big. Herculean. He stomped around the Tucker farm like a bearded giant, never fully understanding the magnitude of his size or why things always seemed to tip over as he passed by. All big, dumb brawn and the brains of a child, which didn't seem all that different from the other kids his age.

Except for the head.

Bubba.

The boy's mama died of a heart attack right there on the birthing table when she saw her baby boy with the second baby's cranium poking out of his chest. She died of fright over the wretched babe that cried with two voices, which was a blessing for her because Bubba needed constant nourishment.

The head sticking out of Mathias's chest had no teeth. It was all baby gums and baby lips and tongue, and it often cried like an infant when Mathias was dog-tired. Or whenever it was hungry.

Bubba had never eaten solid food.

If his mama had lived, she'd have been breastfeeding still, even though Mathias had already had his seventeenth birthday. Papa Tucker bottle-fed both mouths after his sister Loretta (the boy's mama) passed on, pushing the nipple first into Mathias's mouth, and then into the second waiting mouth until both heads fell fast asleep. But as the boy grew and developed teeth (and the second head hadn't), he knew he had to switch to processed baby food.

Even then, Bubba always wanted milk.

Dr. Luther had explained to papa that separation wasn't an option; that because of the second head's positioning right over Mathias's heart, surgery meant the risk that the inbred sombitch that was his second son would likely pass on. And the truth was that papa Tucker couldn't afford the surgery anyway.

Or a funeral.

Mathias stood over the woman tied up in the cattle barn and giggled, the whiskers of his beard curling around a smile of crooked, dirty teeth. His brother Tobias had kidnapped another one, this one a pregnant woman in her late twenties (not that Mathias could tell), and left her there for the boy to have his way with. The woman was unconscious, lashed about the wrists and ankles, and naked as the day was long. Mathias looked down at her, not understanding that the woman was pregnant, thinking that she was just a bit fat the way the hogs got fat every fall before the winter slaughter. Mathias admired the woman's bare skin, the way the dust and hay clung to her sweaty body, the way her breasts swelled and her nipples puckered erect, like pig teats when the sow was ready to suckle her piglets.

"Boobies!" Mathias uttered.

"Feed me," Bubba called from beneath the bib of his overalls.

Mathias unclasped one button and then the other, and the bib of his overalls fell down over his torso. Bubba glanced down at the girl and smiled a big, gummy baby smile.

The woman twitched for a few seconds, and then she opened her eyes and screamed.

Mathias knelt down and placed his mouth on hers. She gagged and gasped and whimpered as he pressed

Bubba's face to her bosom and the freakish head in his chest clamped its mouth on her right tit and began to suckle.

Chapter 2

Tobias Tucker dragged the woman out of the barn, picked up her corpse, and threw it into the bucket-loader of the old Ingersoll tractor. It looked like Mathias had kilt her at some point. He'd merely been trying to silence her, but when he wrapped his giant mitts around the girl's head and shook, he snapped her neck with absolute ferocity. Her naked body jiggled as it settled into the cold steel of the tractor (the swell of her bare breasts and impregnated tummy caused his pecker to twitch, but he didn't dare to do anything about it while Papa Tucker was around), and he found himself wishing the inbred freak that was his brother would just fucking die.

Tobias could have had a lot of fun with this one.

How many times had he fantasized about fucking a pregnant girl? He'd come close enough with Cousin Colleen right after Uncle Herschel knocked her up, but Colleen had been all hormonal and bitchy, and when he tried to place her hand on his cock, she told him if he ever tried something like that again she'd cut it off like a turkey's head at Thanksgiving. But this one in the bucket loader... Good Christ, she was still gorgeous, even with the flies crawling over her dead flesh.

And he was hungry.

While Mathias and Bubba were busy feeding themselves on lust and warm booby milk, Tobias had been out digging the new well. Under the blazing sun, with the shovel's wooden handle gouging and offending the skin of his hands, Tobias had to listen to that freak telling the bitch to "Baa like a sheep," as his inbred penis filled her and his other head gummed and sucked at her mammary.

Papa Tucker was still close by. He'd been mending a fence this morning, and every now and then, he would look over at the barn, waiting to see if Mathias and Bubba had been fed. When Mathias came out of the barn smiling and giggling and buttoning the straps of his overalls (putting Bubba away to catch some sleep), he knew the woman was stone-dead. When he noticed the zipper on the boy's pants was still down, Papa also knew the dead girl had been fornicated with.

Tobias was jealous.

After all, *he* was always the one that had to go out and bring his brother (and the ever-hungry head in his chest) a fresh, new mommy-to-be. And that was always risky as hell. Good Lord forbid he should ever get noticed and arrested and have to spend his life in jail getting raped by all them sodomites with gang tattoos and huge peckers and strange blood diseases.

The girl in the bucket loader was still breathing.

Tobias noticed it just before he turned to climb onto the tractor.

He'd already dug a hole out at the north end of the vegetable field to bury the bitch, right at the edge of the other plots that had become a mass grave, the way third-world drug cartels dug mass graves to dispose of their victims. The back-hoe on the tractor had already accidentally dug up the mangled limbs of one of Bubba's other feeders. The smell had been enough to make Tobias throw up the remnants of his breakfast. Now here was the latest victim, still breathing but motionless due to the broken neck Mathias had inflicted upon her.

Tobias approached the woman in the bucket loader.

He liked the way her engorged tits drooped over her swollen belly.

"How'd you like my brothers?" he asked. He gave her an awful wink. "Looks like Mathias didn't finish the job. Did Bubba suck you dry?"

Tobias bent down and placed his lips on the crippled woman's left nipple. He sucked and felt the warm stream of milk fill his mouth. Even paralyzed, she could still lactate for the baby she would never have. The woman opened her eyes and tried to scream, but the breath in her fractured larynx came out in a raspy whistle.

He opened his eyes and looked into her face as his mouth coaxed the baby milk out of her. After a few mouthfuls, Tobias removed his lips and smiled at her.

"I'm real sorry about this, ma'am. You're awful pretty, and I hate to see you die."

He removed his pocket knife and pulled the blade from out of the handle.

The woman looked at the knife and moaned. Tears spilled from her eyes. From her vagina, a hot stream of urine spilled down her useless legs. Tobias could still see the gobs of his brother's spunk drying across her thighs.

"I'm sorry, but you've got to go. Can't have no Johnny Law come looking for ya!"

Tobias pressed the knife into her left breast and began to hack it off. The flesh severed in rough gashes of pink muscle, capillaries, blood, and milk. He didn't stop until her mammary flopped into the palm of his shaking hand. The woman's eyes went big, and hisses of blood and saliva escaped her dying lips. The fetus in her womb kicked and throbbed in her belly for a few moments, and then it, too, fell silent.

Tobias looked at the severed tit in his hand. He admired the way the areola stood up pert and erect even after the breast had been severed from her body. Bubba had already supped on that nipple, had drunk his share of the warm fluid of life as Mathias had mounted the bitch and stuffed her cunt with his erection. Tobias didn't care. He spat out the plug of tobacco he'd been chawing on, then he lifted the severed breast to his mouth, bit the nipple clean off, and began to chew. He paid no attention to the blood that started to spill down his chin. It mingled with his saliva and tobacco juice, forming a greasy trail that stained his shirt orange.

"Boy, what the hell you doing?"

Papa Tucker had snuck up behind him. Tobias jumped as if he'd just been bitten by a rattlesnake. He turned and faced the old man and held out the bloody tit for him to examine.

"I'm sorry, Papa. I was just hungry. I've been working all day."

Papa reached out and snapped the tit out of his son's hand. He lifted it to his face, gave it a few good sniffs, and smiled.

"Implants," he said. "God, don't they smell purty." He opened his mouth and took a bite. "This one tastes like it was filled with honey." He looked down at the girl in the bucket loader, all blood and dusty flesh beginning to decay in the hot sun. "I bet her pussy-hole tastes like honey, too." He handed the tit back to the boy, lifted his straw hat, and wiped the sweat off his brow.

"I wouldn't go trying to find out," Tobias answered as he watched his idiot brother come lumbering up to them. Mathias had that stupid grin still plastered across his face, and Tobias was certain that, underneath the overall bibs, Bubba probably had one as well. Only Bubba would have that telltale milk mustache smeared across his upper lip, like a hideous puppet in a *Got Milk?* advertisement. "Why can't Mathias bury this one?"

"Because Mathias can't drive a tractor."

Mathias blushed and giggled.

"Daddy, her fuck-hole was all furry like a sheep," he stammered. "I tried to get her to go 'baa,' but she just kept screaming at me. I got scared and tried to get her to be quiet, but I broke her neck."

A noise came from below the bib of his overalls. It sounded like a child's voice, grunting and mumbling.

Papa gave an annoyed look at Mathias and then reached out at his inbred son. He unbuckled the left side of his britches, exposing Bubba's fleshy head.

"What'd you say, boy?" he demanded.

"I said, 'maybe she likes horsies,'" Bubba answered.

Mathias and Tobias both reared back and howled out in laughter.

With one quick, deliberate swing, Papa Tucker slapped the laughter out of both his children's faces. The force of his blow left hot, red hand marks on their cheeks. Tobias dropped the tit onto the dirt and put his hand on his skin.

"What'd you do that for? Now that titty ain't no good to nobody!"

Papa shook his head.

"I should have wrapped your mama in burlap and dumped her in the river the moment she told me she was knocked up," he said. "Curdled cow piss, don't you two complicate my life. Cut off her other booby if you're still hungry. And when you're done, get her corpse buried so she ain't stinking up my farm. I got the banker-man gonna be paying us a visit any day now, wanting to know why I can't pay the mortgage. How's he gonna act if he sees what we've been up to?"

"Sorry, Daddy," the fleshy lump of Bubba's head announced. Even for a deformity, the damn thing had a better brain in him than those lunkheads Toby and Matty. And sure enough, they both hung their heads and also offered an apologetic, "Sorry, Daddy."

Mathias lifted the bib back up and buckled the strap. Tobias bent down and picked the severed tit off the ground. He dropped the fleshy gland into the bucket loader and then wiped the blood on his hand onto the denim of his jeans. He walked over to the tractor's step and went to climb on. He'd half-hoisted himself up into the seat when Mathias called up to him.

"Can I he'p you, if you need he'p and all?"

"Yeah, sure…climb on board, Matty."

"Can I ride with her, up in the bucket?"

Tobias sighed. "That don't make no never-mind by me."

Lee Tucker shook his head. "You idjuts will be the death of me yet. Just make sure you plant her down all the way. I don't want to see her one good titty sticking up out the ground like some of the others you done buried. And I sure don't wanna see no coyotes out digging in our crops once the sun goes down."

Chapter 3

The slick-looking banker dude pulled his car off the road and parked out in front of the barn. Lee Tucker stopped tacking up the new fence wire and watched the sky-blue Mazda glide up to the barn door like a serpent and then nod off into slumber as the banker fella turned off the ignition, opened the door, and slid effortlessly out from behind the wheel. He stood for a second, fishing into the passenger seat for a file of paperwork, and then pulled the door closed.

"Well, shit," he said as he got to his feet. He spat the plug of tobacco out of his mouth, his hand still firmly clutching the shaft of his hammer. The banker noticed him immediately and began making a bee-line toward him. Lee looked down at the hand holding the hammer and smiled as his hand began to twitch. His grip was so tight he could feel the pulse of his blood vessels beneath his sunbaked skin.

"Lee Tucker," the banker fella hollered from twenty paces away. "I represent the Cold Currant Savings and Loan Company."

"I know who you are, son. You're Winston and Bobbi-Jean Gray's boy," Tucker spat. "Who the hell you think you are showing up here in the middle of a work day? Can'tcha see I'm busy?"

The banker fella showed little concern. He closed the remaining paces and held his hand out for Tucker to shake, but when he saw the dirt and sweat on his hand (and the hammer, still locked in a death-clench), he dropped his own hand immediately.

"I'm sorry about that, Mister Tucker, but I'm obligated by virtue of my position as vice president of Cold Currant, to personally deliver all foreclosure documents and legal materials to those persons in default." The banker fella offered a smile that seemed both sad and sinister at the same time. "You're delinquent in your payments, Mister Tucker. Third month in a row. Now, I'm sorry as hell, but you have to take this here information."

Lee Tucker stared down the banker dude but made no motion to take the paperwork. Behind the dude, Tucker could see his two sons riding back up the fields in the tractor. He could see the blood stains on top of the faded green paint of the Ingersoll's bucket loader. He was going to motion for the boys to go away, but instead, he decided to let them come. They would see the banker dude, and the nosey, stupid sonsabitches would want to know what was going on. They would find out anyway, and Tucker liked the idea of safety in numbers.

"I'm serious, Mister Tucker..."

"Call me Lee," Tucker smiled back. "I used to beat up your daddy back in grammar school. Hell, I had my fingers in your mama's honey-pot way back in the summer that she first got her titties. That practically makes us kin, Nelson Gray."

"*MISTER TUCKER*, in thirty days, I will be returning here with Currant County law enforcement officials. If you have not vacated these here premises, you will be forcibly removed as stipulated by state law. Your property and assets will be inventoried and publicly auctioned off to recoup our investments. Now kindly take these here documents and go over them."

The banker fella extended his arm and held out the file. Tucker made no move to accept it. Instead, he watched as his boys drew closer on the tractor. The old Ingersoll roared and sputtered like a wounded animal, puffing and chugging in coughs of toxic diesel smoke. They were almost right on top of him.

"Look, I'm sorry, Mister Tucker, but when you took out your mortgage, you made a contractual obligation with the bank. And you failed on that obligation. It's not my fault or my doing. It's nothing personal."

"Boy, if I were you, I'd just drop that file on the ground and get the fuck out of here while you still can walk."

The smile dropped off the banker's face like shit dropping from a cow's ass. He tossed the file onto the grass, sending a swarm of summer flies and bugs racing in every direction. He turned to leave and just narrowly missed getting scooped up in the bucket of the tractor.

"Hey, watch it, you inbred goon!"

Lee Tucker lunged forward and caught the banker dude by the collar of his white button-down shirt. He spun the boy effortlessly with a twist of his giant, farm-muscled arm so that Nelson Gray, son of Winston and Roberta (who owned a dairy farm not even two miles up the road), was staring down a smile of colored, broken teeth.

"Just because yer mama and daddy wasn't related don't give you the right to insult my boys."

Tobias shut the tractor's engine off and jumped down to the ground. Mathias, the hulking idiot with the second face growing out of his chest, followed silently. The two boys laughed as the banker dude began to squirm in their daddy's clutch.

"Now get off my land," Tucker growled and released his grip. Nelson-the-banker-dude dropped down on his ass, and a second wave of bugs scattered in the heat. Nelson half-crawled, half-rolled until he was out of range of the freakish family behind him before he felt safe enough to get up and sprint to his car.

"They're taking the farm back, ain't they, Papa?" Tobias said. He pulled a handkerchief out of his pocket and wiped the sweat off his forehead. "We shoulda just kilt that sombitch while we had the chance."

"What's gonna happen to us, Daddy?" Mathias said. "Where we gonna live if they take the farm away?"

"Boy, we got bigger problems than that," Lee Tucker answered. "If Nelson Gray comes back here with the law, and they take the farm away, how's it gonna look when the next land-owner plows the fields and stumbles on all them dead girls we got planted out back? Now, I can lie to 'em and say it was all my doing, but I don't think they gonna buy that shit. There's three grown men living out here, and I'm of the age that they ain't gonna suspect I've been kidnapping and diddling them young girls for my own gratification. You two, on the other hand…"

"Daddy, I was just doing what you told me to," Tobias said, looking guilty as hell. He had Loretta's dark, curly hair, but his strong chin and sharp facial features looked just like his own. And at least he wasn't deformed like his other half-wit son. Tobias could have been somebody, could have been respected and important, had he been blessed with better parents. But you're stuck with the hand you're dealt, and you have to play that hand the best you can. For Tobias, that meant keeping the tractor fixed and running, planting and harvesting, and caring for Mathias. God knew, Lee Tucker wouldn't be around forever, and nobody else was going to take care of Mathias. And Bubba.

"We gonna have to dig 'em all up," Lee Tucker finally said. He took his hat off his head and wiped the sweat from his balding pate with his forearm. "Every single one of 'em. We can't keep them here anymore. It ain't safe. If they come to foreclose, we can't have the law finding any dead bodies on our property. Simple as that."

"What's the difference?" Tobias asked. "We got nowhere else to go. If we lose the farm, we got nothing. We got no jobs, no food, and no place to sleep. Daddy, I'd rather die than be forced off the farm."

Mathias nodded. "Me, too, Daddy. This is our home."

From inside the bib of his overalls, Bubba started making guttural noises.

"You okay in there?" Mathias asked the conjoined lump.

Before it could answer, Bubba vomited up a hot stream of chunky, curdled breast milk all down the inside of Mathias's overalls. Mathias felt the puke flow down his stomach, loins, and thighs. It trickled like hot lava until it coursed down over his bare feet. When it finished retching, Bubba began to sob out loud.

"Oh, my sister's hairy asshole," Papa Tucker shook his head in disgust. "Go get yourself a clean pair of britches. Then come on back and help your brother. If you boys really want to make a stand, then we got a lot of work to do. We're gonna have to spill a lot of blood if we're gonna keep this here farm."

Chapter 4

Betty-June Gray was sitting at the lunch counter of the Summer Street Café, waiting for Nelson to meet her for lunch. The air inside the café was hot, almost stifling, despite the incessant whir of the ancient air conditioner behind the counter. Summers in Cold Currant, Mississippi never dipped below sweltering. Even the flies that buzzed angrily at the front windows of the café tended to move slowly to avoid overheating.

She'd suffered morning sickness (wasn't *that* supposed to end after the first trimester?) well into the early afternoon, and yet, somehow, she still mustered the fortitude to crawl out of bed and get chores done around their tiny, one-bedroom apartment before donning her lightest summer dress (which was barely fitting over the bulge of her full-grown tummy) and running her myriad errands before meeting her husband, Nelson, for lunch.

Leave it to Nelson to be running late.

Betty-June was suffering between fits of hunger and nausea. She'd already spent a good hour or so hovering next to the toilet, whoopsing up her first two cups of coffee, and then the eggs and grits she cooked up after Nelson kissed her goodbye and left for work at the bank. Betty-June had cooked him up a much more elaborate breakfast: eggs, bacon, toast with butter and honey, and fresh strawberries she'd bought for him at the farmer's market. With his position as Vice-President of Cold Currant Savings and Loan, she knew Nelson was a man of power and importance—at least in terms of societal position. In reality, Nelson was a tad on the spineless side. And lord knew, he wasn't the best-looking man in Cold Currant.

This was the rub of being Mrs. Nelson Gray: there were far manlier men to be found, but none of them offered the prospect of a decent, struggle-free life here in a town of hardships and desperation. And, of course, there were a whole lot more women willing to take her place if Nelson ever got tired of her and decided to kick her to the curb. And by women, she meant the other townie girls that barely scraped through high school and found themselves stuck on the family farms, hauling in crops of tobacco leaves or watermelons until their backs went bad.

But did she actually love him?

Betty-June was certain that Nelson loved her. Willie

Nelson Gray had a boyhood crush on her through most of high school. And when he returned home from college and she was still working the cash register at the local Piggly Wiggly, he practically swept her off her feet. Not as the dashing Prince Charming out of a fairy tale, but in the way that those people in the Publisher's Clearing House commercials always look so happy when the van shows up to deliver those million-dollar checks. He was an opportunity for *something better*, and she loved him dearly for that. Enough to become Mrs. Nelson Gray. Enough to spread her legs for him and let him fill her belly with his child.

The bell on the café door tinkled, and she turned and watched Nelson walk in from the summer heat. He offered a friendly nod to Laverne, the girl working the lunch counter (who was the same age as Betty-June and spent most of her time giving her dirty looks and then whispering rumors about her to the other waitress that worked the tables), before sauntering over and parking himself on the stool next to her.

"You look better than when I left you this morning," Nelson said before leaning over to give her a peck on the lips. "Sorry I took so long."

"It's okay, sweetie," she lied. "I know you're a very busy man."

Laverne walked over, her pad and pen in hand. "What'll it be today, Mister Gray?"

Betty-June could hear the sarcasm in her voice. The bitch had the gall to mock him when *she* was nothing more than...well, a slave to her job. A job that was going nowhere, while Betty-June was going to have the luxury of being a stay-at-home mom. Of course there would be jealousy.

"Gimme a turkey-and-Swiss on rye and an iced tea. What'll you have, sweetie?"

Nelson was glancing at her, his eyes tracing the skin of her bare neck, working all the way down to her swelling cleavage. Betty-June's tits had been off-limits once they'd grown sore and tender with pregnancy. She still let him diddle her honey-pot, had enjoyed the way it took her mind off the babe growing inside her and the pain and discomfort it brought. She even let him enter her every now and then. (She was always on top; she wasn't taking any chances with the baby.) But the breasts were now off-limits. Decorations only.

Lord knew, she was already dreading the pain it would bring once their newborn began to suckle.

"I'll have the same," Betty-June said, not even bothering to look up at Laverne. Instead, she feigned a performance of looking dreamily into her husband's eyes and smiling shyly as Nelson gazed at her body. *Eat your heart out, bitch,* she thought to herself as Laverne scribbled on the pad and went back into the kitchen to fill their order. For all she knew, Laverne might just spit in their sandwiches as she made them. It didn't matter. Betty-June wasn't sure she was going to eat hers anyway. She was feeling nauseous again.

"I have a surprise for you," Nelson began. "You know the old Tucker farm? The one way out on the River Road?"

Of course, she knew about the Tucker farm. It was one of the oldest farms in the county. It used to be an antebellum cotton plantation that sat right along the banks of the Mississippi River. Nowadays, though, it was a produce farm occupied by a bunch of dirty rednecks. She'd just seen the two Tucker boys at the farmer's market the other day when she went to buy Nelson's strawberries. Their fruits and vegetables always looked fresh and delicious, but she couldn't stand the thought of those two inbred hooligans placing their filthy hands all over her food. And truth be told, she'd rather starve than have to approach them and buy their goods.

"Yes…what about it?"

"Their farm is about to become vacant. Lee Tucker is in arrears on his mortgage, and the bank is going to foreclose. Now, I was thinking it's about time you and I bought our own house…"

"Oh, sugar…I don't know."

"What do you mean? The historical value of that farm alone is worth the investment. And have you ever seen how massive that old plantation house is? We could fit four or five of our apartments inside it. Besides, we need more space for our growing family."

Nelson reached his hand out and placed it on his wife's belly. Beneath her dress, the baby began to kick as if sending its agreement.

"Oh, Nelson, have you ever seen those boys that live there now? Are you really sure you want to live in their home? God only knows what a pigsty it is inside."

Laverne walked out of the kitchen holding a tray

with their sandwiches and drinks. She strolled over and set their plates and glasses in front of them, then raced away to titter about them with the other waitress.

"I've thought a lot about this," Nelson said as he picked up his sandwich. "We can get the house for a song and dance at auction. Having those dirty rednecks occupying the house is only going to bring down the cost for us. And once they're out, we can take out a loan and fix it up however we want. We can restore that old plantation house and drive its value sky-high. Then, if you hate it and don't like living there, we can just sell it and move wherever we want."

Betty-June sighed. She hoisted the pickle off her plate and took a bite. Nelson was already half-way done with his sandwich.

"If it's what you really think we should do," she said, "then, let's do it. But you have to swear to me that the house will be safe and baby-proof by the time I go into labor."

"I swear it, honey. We're all going to be very happy there."

This was the rub of being Mrs. Nelson Gray: Nelson always gets his way.

Chapter 5

"Lord, for this meal, make us truly grateful."

Lee Tucker unclasped his hands and reached for the plate of meat in front of him. All breasts, all white meat, none of it from chickens. It struck him funny for a moment that he counted seven tits on the serving plate, that there always seemed to be an odd number whenever Tobias cooked dinner, but he let the thought pass. Hell, his son worked hard, and if he snatched one off the grill and wolfed it down before his idiot brother could notice, that was fine. Besides, looking at the table (filled with bowls and bowls of cooked vegetables), it wasn't like there wasn't enough to eat.

The new fertilizer he switched to this season was making all the difference.

The crops had never looked so crisp, so bountiful. Glory be, it was like they had to go harvest vegetables every single morning. If he plucked one ripe, red tomato off the vine, it was like two more grew in its place overnight. By midsummer, they had plum-run out of space in the barn's refrigeration room to store all they were harvesting. By then, Lee had Matty on canning detail, sealing up cans and jars of beans, spinach, and tomatoes every evening while Toby cleaned and put away the supper dishes.

And that was the bitch of it. Lee was sitting on the biggest harvest he'd ever had on the farm. But selling at the farmer's market just wasn't bringing in the cash they needed to pay off the mortgage. It brought in *some* money—enough to furnish him with his whiskey and cigarettes—but the capital he needed to sustain the farm was locked up in unsigned contracts with local frozen-goods distributors, and that no-good sombitch Clyde Hamilton at the Piggly Wiggly (who owned two other stores on top of the one in Cold Currant) had signed a supply contract with some farmers *outside* of Mississippi.

And may the ghost of Robert E. Lee cram a bayonet up his ass!

Tobias and Matthias began loading their plates up with food. Matty grabbed up the plate of grilled breasts and plopped two mismatched pieces onto his plate. The larger of the two still had a jiggle to it, and Matty giggled as he took his fork and jabbed at the nipple still attached to the lower portion.

"*Tee hee hee.* Toby didn't cook this long enough."

Lee's hand swung out and slapped the stupid grin off his face.

"Goddamn it, boy! You're almost a man now. Stop playing with your food."

Toby shook his head. "Sorry, brother. I guess my mind was off somewhere else while I was cooking dinner."

Matty winced, rubbing his hand absently where his cheek burned from his daddy's swat. "It's okay, Toby. I'm sure it'll still be delicious."

"We gonna have to move them bodies starting tomorrow morning," Lee announced, dragging his knife through the piece of tit on his plate. He forked the piece to his mouth and began to chew. "I reckon we must have some thirty-odd corpses scattered through our fields. That's gonna take a lot of work. Particularly if we're trying to move 'em in the daytime, where people might see what we's up to if they come a-callin'."

"Where we gonna move 'em to, Daddy?" Toby was heaping a pile of squash onto his plate. He set the serving spoon down, picked up his butter knife, and scooped a huge wad of butter onto the squash.

"I ain't fer sure yet," Lee answered. "I think, for the time being, we just gonna have to haul 'em up to the barn. We can just weigh 'em down and toss them right into the river if we have to. We won't be able to do it all at once, but maybe five every night until they're all gone."

Toby and Matty both nodded as if this plan made all the sense in the world.

Toby looked up from his plate. "The squash is delicious. I mean, it's really, really good. Try some, Matty."

"I don't like vegetables," Matty protested.

Lee Tucker raised his hand to swing again, and then Matty was grabbing the bowl of squash and plopping spoonful after spoonful onto his plate.

"All the vegetables are good this season," Lee said. "It's that fertilizer we got from Roscoe Hunnicut. I think he's mixing processed fish guts into the manure. Maybe he's adding some new-fangled chemical or something. It don't make us no never-mind. All that matters is that shit really works."

"And it stinks to high-hell," Matty interrupted.

"I thought Roscoe said his fertilizer was 100% orgasmic. That means they can't add no chemicals," Toby stammered between mouthfuls. By then, he was working on his own piece of tit.

"Organic, you idiot." Lee dropped his elbow onto the table and palmed his face into his open hand. Christ Jesus, he shoulda shacked up with someone *other* than his older sister. The two had produced a pair of turd-brained dunces.

From somewhere beneath the bib of Matty's overalls, Bubba began to sob. It came slowly at first, muffled, and then grew to an all-out bawl. Matty undid the straps of his overalls and let the bib drop so that Bubba was free. His infantine face cringed at the light until its eyes came into focus, and then he looked around the table.

"Hungry!" it demanded.

Matty clumsily lifted his glass of milk and moved it toward Bubba's lips.

"No, I want *breast milk!*" Bubba demanded.

Lee Tucker leaned forward so that his face was inches away from the deformity in Matty's chest. "How many times do I have to tell you? If Mathias keeps killing the girls we bring him, you don't get breast milk. Okay? You gotta start keeping them bitches *alive* if you want fresh milk every day, just like you would a cow." And then to Mathias, "Do you hear me, boy? Every time you kill 'em, you shut off Bubba's supply. And you make more trouble for us. Look at all the goddamn bodies we now have to dispose of because of you. It's amazing the law ain't figured us out yet. It's a goddamn miracle we all ain't in jail already."

Lee sighed and sat back in his chair. "Toby, do you think you can get out tonight and grab a new one for your brother?"

Bubba whimpered as Matty pushed his glass of milk toward his waiting mouth again. The lump began to drink, and Matty watched it quietly, his face a contortion of guilt and shame.

Toby looked up from his plate. He had a bite-full of tit hanging out of his mouth, the nipple poking out erect with little black char-stripes hashed out across it where the meat had roasted on the grill.

"Daddy, where the hell am I gonna find a pregnant girl at this time of day? It ain't like the town's crawling with knocked-up girls just waiting to be kidnapped. And after this last one, the police are gonna be cracking down hard on anybody who looks suspicious."

Lee Tucker lifted another bite of tit to his mouth

and pushed it in. He chewed on it a moment, deep in thought, and then answered.

"Nelson Gray's wifey is knocked-up. Maybe tonight you could pay 'em a visit."

Tobias Tucker looked up from his plate, his demeanor cool and serious.

"Oh, Daddy... Not Betty-June!"

"You still sweet on that girl?" Lee snarled. "Has that bitch ever even given you the time of day? She ain't never wanted nothin' to do with you. You got to face the fact that she's married to that limp-dick Nelson, and that limp-dick Nelson is trying to take *our* house from us. You hear me?"

"Yes, Daddy."

Tobias Tucker pushed his plate away, stood up, and left the dinner table.

Chapter 6

It was nearly 1:00 a.m. when Tobias got out of bed and began slipping his clothes on. First his jeans (the cleanest ones he owned, which were still soiled filthy since they hardly bothered with laundry anymore), and then a plain black Haynes t-shirt. He sat on his bed and threw on his socks, then his work boots (which were equally soiled). Toby sat on the edge of his bed, looked at his boots for a moment, then decided against them. The imprint treads on the bottom would be easily distinguishable, especially if he had to enter Nelson Gray's home and abduct his wife. Gray was someone important. The law wasn't going to conduct some half-assed investigation this time around.

Especially after Daddy had explained to his idiot brother for the hundredth time that they needed to keep these girls alive if they were to keep Bubba fed. No, sir. The law would be out looking for her, would want to return her alive and safely as possible.

The law would come, and they would shoot first and ask questions later.

We're gonna have to spill a lot of blood to keep this farm!

This was such a terrible idea. They'd be better off just killing Matty and dumping *him* in the river. After all, this was all *his* fault to begin with.

And Daddy's. Lee Tucker is the one that allowed all this to happen. He made *me do this!*

This brought up another option: he *could* always go to the cops. He could rat out his Daddy and his idiot in-bred brother. Just tell them everything, all the way from the start. After all, it had been Daddy that had brought those first few women home, back when Toby was too young to understand what kidnapping even meant.

Tobias wished Mama was still alive.

He never really had the chance to know Loretta Tucker, never had the chance to bond with his Mama/ Aunt. He only knew old black-and-white photos and mementos of the things that had been her life. Like the cross-stitch samplers she used to sew and the mono-grams that adorned most of the blankets and pillows they used. Or the handful of old dresses that still lingered in her closet (the colors now faded, and the cloth festooned with holes where moths had devoured them). Every now and again, he would catch Mathias rummaging through her old clothes. Sometimes he would be sobbing. Other times he would be playing with her undergarments, brushing the cups of her bras against his face or sniffing her panties. Whenever he did this, he could hear Bubba whimpering, "Oh, Mama..."

Toby tugged off the boots and switched to an old pair of his Daddy's shoes. If he had to leave clues behind, why not implicate the old man rather than himself? The shoes were old patent-leather deals, with the soles scuffed perfectly flat on both feet. The shoes were a bit tight on him, but that didn't make him no never-mind. It wasn't like he would wear them forever and ever...

When he was completely dressed, he crept downstairs and snatched the keys to Daddy's pick-up truck, grabbed a piece of jerky from the pantry, and pushed out the kitchen door into the hot, hazy summer night.

He heard the noise the moment he stepped out the door. Toby wasn't sure what it was, other than it sounded like the kind of racket a wounded animal might make when it knows its time has come. He'd heard pigs make the same kind of racket, just as their hind legs were tied and hoisted into the air and the blade came down across their throats.

The noise was coming from out in the fields.

Something had found the bodies.

"Oh, no!" Toby uttered before turning tail back into the house. When he emerged again, he was carrying a shotgun and a flashlight. He turned the light on and began to stalk his way out into the crops.

The bristle of the plants against his thighs as he crept through the rows of vegetables made him nauseous. The ever-present stench of the fertilizer penetrated his nose. It smelled oppressive, unnatural, and made him gag reflexively. He pushed further out into the field. By now, the sound was much closer, more audible. At first, he thought he heard the sound of a baby crying. It sounded like the wail and sob of an infant. No… More than one. It sounded like a *lot* of babies crying. They wailed and gasped and sputtered with that piercing sound only tiny vocal cords can make.

Toby could feel the hackles rise on his skin. The noise was horrific, obscene, like the scent of the manure that repulsed him so. He lifted the flashlight and began to shine it around the rows of vegetation that had grown over the humps of the corpses they'd buried there in the back field.

When Toby saw them, he dropped the shotgun. He stared dumbfounded across the strange vegetation.

They'd filled the earth with dead mothers-to-be. Now their babes grew out of the ground, roped to the earth with slimy green umbilical cords. Dozens of them, with bodies shriveled like tiny pumpkins writhing about in the soil. Tiny arms and legs, with sprigs of green leaves and chutes poking through their bare skin, were kicking and jabbing into the air as these horrid fetuses joined the crops of gourds and rhubarb and carrots.

All of them were screaming. All of them were waiting for breast milk.

Toby swung the flashlight around the crop of baby fetuses, praying this was all just a very bad dream.

Chapter 7

"Daddy, wake up!"

Tobias had run full-gallop back to the house with a chill of terror in his blood-stream that ran so cold it made him shiver. He had dropped the rifle and left it in the field, but he still had the flashlight in his hand, and when Lee Tucker awoke, he felt the light's beam immediately blinding him.

"Boy, what the fuck are you doing?"

"Get up, Daddy. This is serious. You have to come outside and see."

Lee sat upright. "Oh shit! Tell me the police ain't out there."

"They ain't. But you gotta come see. I don't know *what* to do."

Lee reached over and turned on the lamp on his bedside table. When he looked back over at Tobias, he noticed that his oldest boy was crying.

"Get a hold of yourself, boy. Just settle down right now. Then tell me what the hell this is all about."

It took a moment, but Toby eventually collected himself. He grabbed a tissue from the box on the nightstand and blew the flowing snot out of his nostrils (he could almost feel the grime and stench of the dust from the fields come out of him), and then he looked at his father.

"Daddy, there's babies growing out in our field."

Lee's jaw all but hit the floor.

"Have you lost your mind? Did you just have a nightmare or something?"

"No, Daddy...you have to come see for yourself."

Lee Tucker stood up, threw his jeans on, and then he followed Toby out into the field. When they got to the spot where the babies were, he snatched the flashlight from his son's hand and waved it around the field.

It was the same as before; the rows of living baby fetuses sprouting from the earth, growing from the wombs of their dead mothers beneath the soil. They wailed and sobbed at the pain and discomfort of their new lives among the cornucopia of vegetation.

"Holy dog dick!" Lee whispered. He shined the light over the shotgun on the ground. "Did you leave this out here on the ground, boy?"

"I got scared, Daddy."

Lee turned and punched his son square in the jaw.

Toby dropped back on his ass into a wad of cucumber vines, and then he immediately jumped back to his feet in case something in the vines tried to wrap its fingers around him.

The older Tucker leaned over and snatched up the shotgun. He opened the chamber to see if it was loaded, closed it, pumped the weapon, and fired into the crop. A vegetable infant exploded, sending a rain of blood across the field and splattered the skin of both Tuckers.

"It's the fertilizer, ain't it, Daddy? They used chemicals in it. It ain't orgasmic at all!"

Lee stood among the crop of wailing infants. The noise was growing deafening. In all his years, he never heard such a clamor.

"What are we gonna do?" Tobias was blubbering now. He was trying to wipe the blood off his face. The blood smelled very much like the fertilizer.

"Oh, my bleedin' hemorrhoids...I can't believe what I'm seeing," Lee said. "I'll tell you what we got to do. We need to haul the woodchipper out the barn and get it on over here. Then we got to harvest all these... things...and get rid of 'em. We can't have living babies growing in our fields. Go wake your brother up and get him out here. I want these things gone before sun-up."

Chapter 8

Tobias and Mathias spent the night working out in the field. At first, Toby thought that Matty might be a little overcome about the idea of harvesting the vegetable babies and dumping them through the wood chipper, but Matty actually didn't seem to mind. He lumbered out into the field under the night sky and, with Toby holding the flashlight for him, proceeded to cut through the green umbilical cord-stalks with an old lock-blade knife. Without so much as a sigh, the idiot brute plucked up the weeping plant-babes and chucked them unceremoniously into the chipper.

What sprayed out the back of the chipper was a bloody, pulpy mess of goo that stank just as bad as the fertilizer. At first, the pile of pulp was small, but it grew and grew with every babe that went through the machine. And all the while, the din of weeping infants grew less and less until Mathias was clutching the last one by its ankles. Without a thought in his head, he tossed the last one into the chipper (face first) and watched as it disappeared into a bloody spray from the back.

When it was over, Tobias shut the chipper off, threw up, and then staggered out of the field. When he reached the grass, he passed out.

The first rays of dawn's sunlight were just stretching out over the Tucker Farm.

Chapter 9

"Y'all get up now, son."

Tobias felt the kick to his stomach, swift, blunt, and then felt the wind rush out of his lungs as he writhed into consciousness. He rolled around on the ground for a minute, gasping for air.

"C'mon, now…before a cottonmouth decides to nest in your asshole. You've slept long enough."

Toby sat upright, still gasping and whimpering. "What'd you do that for, Daddy? You didn't have to kick me."

Lee Tucker adjusted his hat, wiping the sweat off his brow as he did. "No, I reckon I didn't, but it sure felt good. It's almost ten o'clock. Mathias loaded the truck for you while you was sleeping. Git your ass on down to the farmer's market and try to sell some of them vegetables. And if you make enough money, I want you to stop at the liquor store and buy me some whiskey."

"Is Matty coming with me?"

"He's been up all night, ever since them babies… well, ever since he woke up. He's been out harvesting all morning. I want him to catch some shuteye now, or him and Bubba will be up all night tonight."

"You could come with me. You ain't doin' nothin' today. When's the last time you came down to the farmer's market?"

Lee Tucker spat a huge wad of tobacco out of his mouth, then dragged his arm across his lips to wipe them off.

"Well, I just as soon *NOT* go to the market, if you don't mind. I been doing this shit long enough. I spent years dragging produce down to the farmer's market while you and your brother stayed home and pissed your pants 'cause you wasn't smart enough to go use the outhouse. It's a goddamn miracle the two of you never kilt each other while I was away. Besides, I got to take a ride up to Roscoe's place and talk to him about his fertilizer. I want to know what the hell he's spiking his cow shit with, find out if it ain't secretly poisoning us. He's got some explainin' to do."

Lee started off toward the house. He only got about twenty steps away before he turned around. Enough time for Tobias to stand up and shake the dirt and loose grass off his clothes.

"...And if you see Betty-June Gray while you're out today, see if you can't just invite her over for dinner. Bubba's got to eat, or he'll be crying like a sombitch all night."

Tobias looked down at his clothes. He was still in the jeans and black t-shirt he'd thrown on when he'd dressed to kidnap that Gray bitch, before the whole baby incident had... Well, before the mess. He gazed back into the field, sweeping his eyes across the lush vegetation he and his brother had planted and sewn. The wood chipper was gone. The monstrosity that was his brother must have hauled the gargantuan piece of machinery back to the barn all by himself, a task that he could never have accomplished alone. From his viewpoint, he could not see the huge pile of bloody flesh-pulp where they'd ground up all those vegetable babies into hamburger meat, and that was good because it would have made him throw up to see it. Maybe Daddy had his brother fetch a wheelbarrow and scoop it all up and cart it away somewhere.

As it were, the morning buzzards were already hovering and circling over the field.

If he had the time, he'd have fetched Daddy's shotgun and spent the day blasting the poachers away.

Toby made his way back to the house. He walked inside and felt the stifling heat that was already generating within the kitchen. Toby made his way over to the sink, turned on the faucet, and began splashing handfuls of cold water into his face. The kitchen was filled with sunlight, accentuating the splotches of baby blood that still coated his skin. He pulled his shirt off and began to wash himself.

A wave of snores poured in from the living room. Mathias had fallen fast asleep on the couch, not bothering to pull his work boots off. When Toby glanced in on him, he could see the blood stains all over his boot skins. Matty drew in huge swatches of air as he breathed, producing a noise that sounded like a buzzsaw cutting through hickory wood. From inside the bib of his overalls, Bubba was sobbing and whining, "I'm hungry! I'm so, so hungry!"

Tobias threw on a clean shirt, pulled an ice-cold beer from the fridge, and made his way out to the truck.

It was going to be a hell of a shitty day.

CHAPTER 10

Another shitty day beginning with morning sickness.

Betty-June had gone back to bed after Nelson left for work. At least he hadn't sauntered over in his "I'm-the-man-of-the-house" routine and shut off the air conditioner, reminding her for the umpteenth time that it cost money to run that thing all day and that they should only use it at night to keep the house comfortable so they can both sleep (which translated to: use it only when *I'm* at home). She usually chuckled in her "You know what's best" counter-routine, letting him shut it off for the morning, then turning the damn thing right back on after he left for work.

Nelson could be such a jerk sometimes. But not

this morning, not after he had to endure watching her hovering above the toilet every few minutes and barfing up everything she'd eaten, all the way back to last week's fried chicken dinner. Of course, that was an exaggeration, but that was how it felt as she was tossing her cookies, then watching her husband fixing his tie through her tear-soaked eyes, then puking more, then watching him standing in front of the mirror next to her, grooming himself like a goddamn peacock.

"You should go back to bed and get some rest," he'd said. "You and the baby both need it."

Well, thank you, Mister Sensitive, she thought, dabbing at her mouth with a square of toilet paper before flushing away her mess. *That was my plan all along!*

But lying in bed was doing nothing to help with the nausea, and she was growing a bit bored. What few friends she had were all off at their crappy day jobs, trying to make a few bucks to feed their own crappy children. And mama was still in Galveston, still shacked-up with that Mexican rodeo cowboy she'd fallen for right after her and her father divorced.

She was *trapped.* Trapped in this fun little world of isolation that married life blessed her with, trapped in the web of being Mrs. Nelson Gray. She felt like a spider, all gross and bloated, waiting to be free of this baby pod that grew inside her. She pictured a spider in her mind, wrapping huge tufts of silky webbing around her egg-sack, wondering how long before her mate would return home and tell her it was okay to turn the air conditioner back on now, and why don't you fix me some dinner while you're at it?

Stop it! Betty-June told herself. *You just stop it right now. Stop feeling sorry for yourself. Stop treating yourself like a baby. You're not helpless, and you're NOT a prisoner.*

She stood up, hoisted off her nightgown, and looked at her body in the mirror above her dresser.

Her tummy was enormous. It bulged out across her hips and over her panties in jiggling swaths of flab. Her belly button had gone from an innie to an outie, nesting amid a plane of stretch marks that cracked and branched out like parched clay. She looked horrid.

And she was lactating again. Droplets had formed over the skin of her puckering nipples. Pregnancy had changed the size and shape of her tits, and not for the better (not that Nelson would complain about *that*). Betty-June scowled at herself in the mirror, realizing that she was beginning to resemble a big, fat sow.

Betty-June dressed quickly, then made her way to the kitchen to grab a bite to eat, but the nausea returned. Instead, she grabbed a bottle of water, picked up her purse from the kitchen table, and slid the bottle inside it. Then she retrieved her keys and sunglasses and made her way out the door.

I'm NOT a prisoner, she told herself as she climbed behind the steering wheel of her Jeep and drove off to the farmer's market.

Chapter 11

Lee Tucker drove the old Ingersoll tractor the mile-and-a-half up the road to Roscoe Hunnicut's farm, watching the gas gauge hover just a cunt-hair above the red "empty" line. He could have had Tobias drop him off in the pickup truck on his way to the farmer's market, but the idea of walking home soured him, particularly in this wave of oppressive summer heat. With the tractor, he didn't have to walk, but also, the burning diesel clouds provided a touch of relief over the horrid scent of manure Roscoe's cows incessantly produced.

That, and the odor from the fertilizer, he thought. *It's making our own farm stink just as bad.*

As he neared the dirt road turn-off that led to Roscoe's Farm, Lee could see the old man out in the pasture, tending to one of his cows. The animal was down on its side, trying to pick its head up off the ground as Roscoe worked feverishly behind it. Lee turned the corner and drove up the road, then shut off the tractor just outside the pasture gate.

"Good morning, Lee," Roscoe called. "I'll be with ya in a minute."

Lee jumped down from the tractor, climbed the gate into the pasture, and joined him.

The cow was in bad shape.

"What the hell happened here?" Lee asked. He reached into his pocket and produced his pouch of chewing tobacco. He opened the pouch, whipped out a plug, and stuck it between his teeth and cheek.

"Rattlesnake got her. Sometime this morning. Much too late for me to do anything about it."

Roscoe nodded over to a patch of ground next to the cow. A rattler at least four feet long was dead next to the animal. The cow must have stepped on it inadvertently, then suffered the wrath of its fangs as the snake tried to protect itself. Eventually, the cow must have trampled its head because the snake's skull looked pulverized.

The cow let out with a long, reproachful low.

"Roscoe, ya got to put that bitch out of her misery. Can't ya see she's suffering?"

"I ain't got no ammunition for the rifle," the old man sighed. "I used it all up a couple nights ago. Me and Del Murphy was out drinking beers and shooting at the empty bottles. I just ain't got around to driving into town and picking up new bullets."

Lee Tucker looked down at the dying animal, and for the tiniest trace of a moment, he felt genuine remorse for the beast. The moment passed, and then Lee fished down into the sheath on his belt for his lock-blade knife, withdrew the tool, and stabbed the heifer in the throat with a quick, powerful burst. The cow glanced at him in surprise and then offered the man a look of true gratitude (as much as a beast can offer) as its life slipped away.

Roscoe watched silently, then patted him on the back when it was over.

"Thank you, Lee," he said. "You're a real friend."

"Yeah, well...I'm sorry as hell for the loss. We can't afford to be losing our livelihood nowadays."

"No, we certainly can't. What can I do for ya?"

Lee lifted his hat, wiped away the sweat from his brow, and said, "That fertilizer you sold me is working real good."

Roscoe spat a wad of tobacco juice, phlegm, and saliva next to the dead cow. He stood up and nodded over yonder to the west field. "Well, shit... It don't take no rocket gynecologist to see that. Look how green that field is. The last time I remember ever seeing a field that green was way back when my granddaddy owned this farm. Now, just look at it! This'll be the first bumper crop I ever raised."

"It's a dandy, all right. But what I want to know is just what the hell you added to that cow flop you sold me. And don't try to tell me you ain't addin' something, because if you do, I'm gonna whoop your ass from here to Jackson. You hear me?"

Roscoe spat again.

"Lee, I didn't add nothin'. That's the God's honest truth."

Lee Tucker took a step toward the old-timer and lifted a hand as if to slap him. Roscoe retreated a step.

"I swear it, Lee," Roscoe protested. "I didn't add a cotton-pickin' thing, I'll tell you what! Lookee over yonder at the river." Roscoe lifted a shaking hand and pointed at the muddy blue serpent that cut through the landscape. "Last November, the Atkins Chemical Company got sued by the state for dumping their waste in the water and pollutin' the river. Now, that was going on years ago, back when your daddy was still working your farm. And all those chemicals got buried all along the bottom of the river. For years, the river has been depositing silt and mud on top of those chemicals. Just covering that shit all over and burying it, just like nature intended. But with that lawsuit, the folks at Atkins now have to dredge up all that toxic shit off the bottom of the river and dispose of it properly. I think when they started raking that shit up, it re-polluted the water."

Lee's jaw dropped. "The river's toxic," he whispered. "Thank God! Thank God our drinking water comes from a natural spring well. Great balls of fire! We could all be getting cancer from drinking that stuff."

Roscoe sighed and took another quick step backward. "Just think for a minute, Lee. You may not be drinking it, but my cows do. And their shit is what's fertilizing the crops around here. Yours *and* mine! How safe do you think it is if we're eating what we're growing with it?"

A stunned look came over Lee Tucker's face. "Oh, you sombitch!" He took the last few steps between himself and Roscoe Hunnicut and let his hand fly. He felt the sting against his palm as his open hand connected with the stubbly chin of the old geezer. Roscoe took it like a man and stood his ground.

"T'ain't my fault, Lee," he said as his hand gently caressed his sore face. "I didn't make 'em dredge up the river. And I sure as hell didn't tell the state to make 'em do it. Far as I'm concerned, they shoulda left that shit alone. Mother Nature already covered up all them chemicals and made the river safe again. But my cows got to drink, and most days, the river is all I got."

Lee turned in anger, lifted his foot, and stomped his workboot down hard onto the dead cow. Bovine ribs shattered under his assault. "Fuck!" he shouted. "Fuck! Roscoe, I'm already fixin' to lose my farm to the bank. That crop is about all I got for income. How's it gonna be if people suddenly break out in cancer, and they trace it back to what I've been selling 'em? And what about my boys? What'll I do if they get cancer and die on me?"

"I don't know what to tell ya, Lee. Chances are, I ain't gonna live long enough to see it anyway. My tap water comes from the river. I've been drinking that shit all along." Roscoe heaved a sigh and turned toward the cow. "Now, if that's all you meant to ask me, you ought to be on your way now. I got to bury this here cow before it rots out here in the sun."

Lee Tucker climbed up on the tractor and turned the key. Without being asked, he lowered the bucket loader into the dirt and began bulldozing a hole to bury the animal. As he used the machine to push the carcass in, he found himself wondering if the animal was pregnant and if old man Hunnicut was going to come out here the next morning and find a baby calf sprouting through the ground.

All around him, the fetid stench of death and fertilizer prevailed.

Chapter 12

The sun was up high overhead, sweltering around the swatch of ground inside the Cold Currant Farmer's Market. Tobias drove the old pickup truck into the lot and backed it behind one of the few open picnic tables. The tables formed a long line along the back of the lot, roughly the size of a football field, with green-and-white-striped canvas canopies stretched over poles above them. On weekends, this same lot became the town flea market, but for the rest of the week, the local farmers dragged their wares here to sell. Even now, as Tobias backed in his Daddy's truck, he could see the old, familiar faces.

He parked the truck, climbed out of the cab, and set to unloading the baskets of fresh vegetables—cucumbers, tomatoes, green beans, radishes, etc.—from the truck's bed. Matty had filled each to the brim before heaving them into the back of the truck. Tobias worked quickly, setting the baskets out in the most appealing display he could. It didn't take long for all the shoppers to start making their way down to his table.

"I don't know how y'all are doing it..." Bob Wilson, the guy at the table directly to his left, commented. "...but you've been bringing in the freshest produce all year long."

He indicated with a nod down the line of tables, where most of the other farmers' produce looked stale and withering in the sun, their colors bland and unappealing. Toby's first customer was already grappling with a clear plastic bag and stuffing in bright-yellow summer squash, all the while "ooh-ing" and "ahh-ing" over the mouthwatering vegetables.

"...and you're killing off business for the rest of us. T'ain't right at all!"

Tobias smiled. "Hey, we just grow it. We got no say in who buys it."

The feeling was new to him. Almost alien. Tobias Tucker was not one to know and understand what pride felt like. It was as foreign a concept to him as speaking a foreign language. He only knew that the other farmers were beginning to grow envious, and that this crowd of shoppers had *actually* been waiting for him to arrive to purchase their produce. It made him feel good enough to forget all about the baby harvesting and what had happened earlier that morning on the Tucker farm.

A good, solid half-hour of brisk, lucrative business had passed when he saw her out of the corner of his eye. Betty-June Gray drove into the parking lot, parked her car, and then pulled her enormous belly out from behind the wheel. She wobbled her way upright, closed her door, and began waddling toward the tables. There was the briefest moment when she noticed him staring at her from around the line of customers at his table. Their eyes met, just long enough for her to size him up and dismiss him, and then she was waddling off to the far end of the lot.

The pride he'd been feeling was gone that quickly.

"Oh, you stuck-up bitch," he muttered.

"What did you just call me?" The woman directly in front of him stopped stuffing carrots into her plastic baggie and stared at him with her jaw hanging.

"Not you, ma'am. I'm so sorry. I was thinking about somebody else!"

Betty-June felt nothing but disgust as the Tucker boy admired her from over behind the table. It creeped her out to feel his eyes roving over her pregnant body. It made her feel gross, unattractive. She was only a few years older than Tobias, but she had known him from way back in grade school, before he reached the dropout age and did exactly that. The Tuckers had their own reputation in Cold Currant. They were known to "stick to their own" in terms of family life. But even then, way back on the school bus, she could feel the boy's eyes stealing glances of her, watching her motions and the way her body developed with age. He was a pervert. And here he was, a full-blown man in his own right, still ogling her, still trying to rape her with his eyes and his mind. Never an ounce of decency or respect. And now that she was Mrs. Nelson Gray, decency and respect felt like something that was mandatory.

Didn't it?

So how come she didn't feel decent?

Because you didn't earn *it by marrying Nelson. You* whored *it from him. Deep down, you're still no better than Tobias Tucker! You're just luckier.*

The thought made her nauseous.

She waddled her way to the far tables of the market and began her shopping. Only the wares at each table made the nausea even worse. The stench of semi-rotting vegetables, the hordes of flies that clustered and bragged in dull hums in the summer heat, the pleading in the eyes of all these farmers as she approached, and the desperation that came off them in waves as radiant as the summer sun as she passed without purchasing anything. There was nothing here but Cold Currant misery in the form of underdeveloped produce.

Betty-June passed by most of the tables, not bothering to stop and purchase anything, not bothering to look up at the farmers and offer a polite, "Hello." It was almost akin to social suicide when she thought about it. She was one of their own, after all. Now here she was, looking down on them, knowing that many of these people were in dire straits with the very man she married at the very bank he was working for, which made her unpopular. For her to snub them, to not even dignify their existence, made her an enemy. It made her wonder what was holding them back from picking up the rotten vegetables and hurling them at her.

"Hi, Betty-June!"

She looked up and realized that she'd made it all the way down to Tobias Tucker's table. She'd meant to cut short and head back to her car before she reached his table, but she'd been so lost in thought that she practically waddled her swollen belly right into it. When she heard her name called, it jolted her back to reality.

"Ya ain't purchased anything yet, I noticed. Well, I still got plenty of fresh vegetables. I can't help but notice that you're eating for two and all." Tobias swept his dirty hand over the tops of the baskets, indicating that she should take a gander at all the good-looking produce he still had to sell.

"Oh, no thanks," she said, almost to herself. "I suppose I ain't very hungry today."

"Whaddaya mean you ain't hungry? You got to eat, girl. You wouldn't want your baby to go hungry, would you? Why, he'd get born all fucked-up or something if you don't eat good and proper."

"I have to go," she whispered.

Betty-June turned toward her car and began walking.

"You think you're better than us, don'tcha, Betty-June?" Tobias hollered from behind her, loud enough

59

for the other farmers and shoppers to hear. "You must reckon you're now the Queen of Cold Currant, now that you married that little faggot, Nelson."

She stopped and turned toward Tobias. The crowd went silent as she marched her way back up to the table and stared him down.

"My husband is a good man," she hissed. "And let me just tell you something, Tobias Tucker. My husband and I are going to *OWN* your land once the bank forecloses for good. You just mark my words. You Tuckers are gonna skitter outta Cold Currant like the rats you are, and we're gonna turn your farm into *OUR* kingdom. And, yes, I *am* better than you, you inbred *freak!*"

With that, she turned and marched off to her car.

Any pride Tobias had been feeling was dead inside him, replaced with a seething hatred for Betty-June. He couldn't wait to steal her away from Nelson and hand her over to his freak brother. When it was over, they would shove her and her baby through the wood chipper. All he had to do was wait for nightfall.

Chapter 13

Nelson Gray parked the car just down the road from the Tucker farm, grabbed his camera, and climbed out. He held the camera up and began shooting photographs of the antebellum plantation house that stood nestled between the rows of weeping willows along the flats at the edge of the property. Behind the house were acres of farmland, now lush with growth and vegetation. Nelson could smell the foul tang of manure from the crops. He retched for a moment and decided that breathing through his mouth might be the better option.

He crept closer, firing the camera as he moved. The house's structure seemed to be fairly intact. Yeah, the paint was old, flaking, tinted a mildewed green toward the northern side, but that could be scraped and painted over in a week's time. He zoomed in with the lens and snapped off a few more photos, noticing the old, wavy panes of glass in the windows (not energy-efficient at all; those would have to be replaced) and the dilapidated shingles on the roof.

It was as if nobody had cared for the house in a long, long time.

"Fucking freaks. Y'all got no pride in yourselves. Can't even care for the pigsty you live in."

Nelson crept closer still. He noticed that Lee Tucker's pickup truck was gone, as was the tractor. It looked as if nobody was even home.

Would they have all gone to the farmer's market?

To market, to market, to buy a fat pig.

Hearing the nursery rhyme in his head made him chuckle. He had no idea why it would just pop into his head, but there it was.

Home again, home again, jiggety-jig.

He was going to love being a daddy. He and Betty-June had made it a point to *not* learn the sex of their child. Betty-June insisted that Dr. Long, instead, write the sex of their child down on a piece of paper, put it in an envelope, and just hand it to them. That way, if the suspense became too great for them, they could just tear open the envelope and find out. And since they didn't have a nursery for the baby yet anyway, it wasn't as if they had to worry about decorating it according to the baby's gender.

Now, glancing down at the house, he wondered which room would be the nursery. That was the room that was going to be redone first (Betty-June had insisted and had already procured a handful of her girlfriends to help strip off any old wallpaper and repaint the walls when the time came). He wondered what the rest of the house looked like inside as well. He found himself wondering if he could perhaps find a blueprint of the house, maybe at the Cold Currant library or the Department of Records at the Town Hall. It couldn't be that difficult…

But he was *here*, and he wanted to know *now*…

The Tucker vehicles were nowhere in sight, nor was there any sign of them inbred farmers out in the fields or near the barn. He supposed he could just go down and knock at the door. And if nobody was home…

I'll just peek inside. Nothing more than the first floor of the house. I'll just snap a few pictures and then be on my way. They'll never even know I was there!

The shovel came down hard and flat against the back of Nelson's head. He dropped the camera, staggered for a moment as his knees buckled below him, and then he was toppling to the ground. Nelson had just enough time to look up at Mathias as he lifted the shovel a second time and brought it down, curved side forward, into the lower portion of his face. Nelson screamed as the cartilage in his nose snapped and his teeth flew out in a spray of crimson and pearly whites. His vision filled with stars and then fizzled to black as consciousness fled away.

Mathias picked up the banker man, heaved him over his shoulder, and then grabbed the camera and the shovel. He lumbered off toward the barn under the intense heat of the sun.

Chapter 14

"Boy, it looks like you are in a world of hurt."

Nelson groaned out loud and opened his eyes. His face throbbed with electrical impulses that radiated between a dull throb and the burn of hot pins and needles. He could see just by glancing down his face that his nose was crooked and swollen, could see the purple-yellow stain of bruised skin in the blur of his watering eyes. He couldn't see beyond that, but he could feel the trickle of blood where his mouth and chin were. Nelson ran his tongue along his gums and could feel the gaps where his teeth used to be. Some had been knocked out completely. Others were fractured into jagged spindles and pricks that scratched his tongue as he moved it. Nelson groaned again and looked up.

Lee Tucker was standing over him. Behind him was the younger of the Tucker boys. What was his name? Matthew?

"Just what the fuck did you think you was doin', snooping around our home and taking pictures with that fancy camera of yours? Did you think you wouldn't be noticed?"

The Tucker boy held up his camera. It was the Sony digital camera that he had bought for Betty-June for Christmas, just after they discovered that they were pregnant. Nelson could see the spatter of his own blood across the telephoto lens.

"My cam...my cam..." Nelson stuttered, blood spraying from his mouth with each word. His vision was still hazy, and his brain ached as he tried to swim back to reality. He'd meant to reach up and take the camera and realized that his hands were lashed securely behind his back.

They'd brought him into the barn and tied him up.

Nelson rolled his head to the side and saw his Mazda parked at the rear end of the barn. Of course, they'd already moved his car off the road and hid it away from the world.

His eyes widened.

Did anybody even know he was *here*? Had he told anybody where he was going during his lunch break, or was he operating covertly, not telling anybody that he was off to the Tucker farm to take a few photographs and have himself a little look-see over the new property he was about to acquire for himself and Betty-June?

Betty-June.

Oh, shit!

"My wife!" he whimpered. "My wife knows where I am. She'll call the police!"

Lee Tucker laughed and spat a wad of tobacco juice onto the floorboards of the barn next to where Nelson was sitting.

"Oh, I wouldn't go worrying about that if I was you. Betty-June's on her way." Lee smiled a terrible, self-amused smile. "She'll be here any minute. But you ain't gonna be around long enough to see her."

Mathias heaved the camera at the wall of the barn. It smashed with obscene velocity against the wooden beams and ruptured in a spray of metal and plastic. The sound made Nelson flinch. He wept and trembled as his bladder released. Mathias pointed at the stream of urine flowing from between the banker's legs and laughed.

"Now, let's see… What was it you told me about taking away my farm? About the 'power vested in ya'? Well, I wanna see that power right now, son. I wanna see you use that power to get yourself outta this mess. 'Cuz your life kinda depends on it right now, boy."

Lee Tucker reached into his knife sheath and pulled out his lock-blade. He opened it up in front of the banker and showed him the blade up close. There was still blood on it from when he'd stabbed Roscoe Hunnicut's dying cow.

Nelson wept openly. Tears streamed down his face, and snot flowed from his broken nose. His chin quivered.

"I can help you keep your farm," he stammered.

"I can arrange for the bank to forgive your debt. Just let me go, and I can make your mortgage disappear. It'll be like nothing ever happened."

"I think we both know it's too late for that," Lee interrupted. "By now, you've already notified the Sheriff's office and set an appointment date for them to come evict us. They already know. But what they *don't* know is that you came here today to spy on us. It wasn't on their calendar at all for today." Lee spat again. "You already set the wheels in motion, son. Now those wheels are gonna run you down."

Lee lunged forward and buried the knife into the soft part of Nelson's belly. It was fast, so fast that Lee had already withdrawn the knife before the pain registered. Blood came spurting out of the wound. Nelson howled out in pain.

There was a new voice, one Nelson hadn't heard before. It almost sounded like the voice of a child. He tried to silence his whimpering and groaning so that he could hear it better.

"I wanna see! I wanna see!"

Nelson opened his tear-filled eyes and watched as the younger Tucker boy unhooked the bib of his overalls. And then the face of a deformed infant was sticking out of the hulking retard's chest. The babe's head smiled at him as Nelson began screaming at the top of his lungs.

He screamed and kept screaming 'til Lee Tucker lunged again and slit his throat. His screams continued as a hoarse, gurgling whisper until the life drained right out of him.

Chapter 15

It was well after dark when Betty-June heard the front door open, and then slam shut unceremoniously. She'd been in bed for most of the day, still trying to erase from her mind the scene that had played out at the farmer's market. She could still feel that filthy Tucker boy ogling her and hear him trying to verbally bring her down to his level. It had made her feel disgusting, and she'd found herself crying all the way back to their apartment.

And as if that wasn't enough, the baby was restless. She could feel it squirming and shifting inside of her. Even as she showered (with water hot enough to turn her skin pink, she was that desperate to clean herself off from the farmers market), she could feel it inside her belly, most likely turning to make its exit through her birth canal.

This might be it, she thought. *Baby could be coming tonight. I'll just wait until Nelson gets home, and then we can go to the hospital and check in.*

Nelson was unusually quiet. By now, he should have hollered out his customary, "Honey, I'm home!" As always, Betty-June had placed his martini glass inside the freezer and his dinner in the oven (lasagna tonight, with a loaf of homemade garlic bread on the rack just beneath), everything perfect and waiting for Mr. Nelson Gray to arrive. It might have been the 1950s in the Gray apartment, with Nelson living out his little *Ozzie and Harriet* routine to the best of his liking. Wasn't that what bank vice-presidents did? How long would it be before his sweet disposition changed, before Nelson (the effeminate, mild-mannered banker) suddenly became the domineering, callous husband? The kind that might slap her to remind her just who her daddy was if she inadvertently *forgot* to chill his martini glass or burned dinner.

Wasn't that change happening already? Wasn't she already on a short leash?

Betty-June shivered at the thought.

"Nelson? Nelson, baby, is that you? How was your day?"

I could have found a way, she thought, adjusting the covers on the bed so that they didn't feel so suffocating. *I didn't* have *to marry him. I could have tried harder in school. I could have gone on to college and became a* somebody *just like he did. I gave up! Just like Mama did. Just like* everyone *does in this god-forsaken town.*

70

"Nelson? Come give me a kiss 'hello.' I missed you today."

She could hear the sound of footsteps in the kitchen. She could hear the refrigerator door opening, could hear the sound of a bottle cap being removed from a beer bottle (*Nelson's drinking one of* my *Budweisers? When did that start happening?*) and then the bottle cap being tossed carelessly onto the countertop.

"Honey, are you all right? Did you have a bad day at work?"

She could hear his footsteps coming down the hallway.

"Nelson, I think our baby's coming. My water hasn't broke yet, but I'm pretty sure I'm gonna go into labor soon. Nelson?"

Tobias Tucker burst through the bedroom door. He was all lecherous smile and filthy hands. He tipped the bottle back, guzzled down the beer, and then flipped the bottle over in his hand like a weapon.

"How 'bout that," he sneered. "I'm gonna be a daddy!"

Betty-June turned to the bedside table and tried to reach the telephone, but Tobias closed the gap between them with terrible speed and ferocity. He raised the empty beer bottle and then brought it down across the back of her head.

She felt her mind melting into darkness as he picked her up and carried her out the door.

Chapter 16

"I wanna eat! I wanna eat! I'm soooo hungry."

Betty-June opened her eyes and screamed.

She was naked and flat on her back, with her hands tied to a wooden barn post and her legs spread apart and tied to the rails of some kind of animal stall. It was dark inside the barn, save for the one overhead light cupped in the shiny, aluminum fixture. The light didn't so much illuminate as it did create awkward focal points and terrible shadows.

And it was hot. Ungodly hot, and dry and dusty. She could feel dust and hay beginning to stick to her bare, sweaty skin. She glanced down her naked body, now fully comprehending just how compromised and vulnerable she was; the way her breasts jiggled as she sobbed and quivered, and her pregnant belly in full revolt, ready to expel the baby inside her. Her belly eclipsed just about everything below it, but she was certain her legs and crotch were just as exposed as the rest of her body. They hadn't even offered her the dignity of a blanket beneath her bare ass. She could feel the skin of her cheeks wiggling across the wooden floorboards, catching splinters and rough patches that hurt like hell.

"I'm sooo hungry," the voice insisted. It sounded like a frightened child. Were there others here, being held hostage like she was? If there were, they were being deathly quiet.

"Hello?" Betty-June stammered. "Is there anybody here with me?" A fresh river of tears began to stream down her face. "Please! Somebody please answer me. I need help!"

"…sssoooooo hungry! I want her boobies!"

Betty-June turned her head and looked toward where the voice was coming from. She turned just in time to see Mathias unclip the bib of his overalls and let it fall to reveal Bubba's face in that terrible light. Mathias grinned as he knelt between her spread legs. Bubba smiled as well, and tendrils of baby drool passed through his lips and down his deformed chin. The drool spattered across her bare belly.

"Boobies!!!"

She screamed as Bubba clamped his mouth around her nipple and began to suckle. She screamed and screamed until she strained her vocal cords.

"Baa like a sheep for me," the freakish brute whispered, unzipping the fly on his overalls and pulling out his manhood. "Baa for me, or I'm gonna hurt ya real, real bad!"

As Mathias's penis plunged inside her, her voice gave way to terrified gasps. After a while, she closed her eyes and prayed for it to be over.

Betty-June cried as her water broke. She could feel the inbred Tucker boy's weight pressing down on her belly, pushing her baby further down her birth canal to where his penis was ramming against her cervix. She wept and tried to let her mind fly away, fly off to better times where her Mama and Daddy were still in love and the world still seemed like a big, magical place.

Chapter 17

At some point, she lost consciousness.

When she woke up again, the Tuckers were all surrounding her. The one that had raped her (the one with the deformed baby head sticking out of his chest) was by her feet. He'd fixed his overalls so she couldn't see the deformed baby head, and that was a blessing. If she saw it again, she was sure she would have died of fright. The other boy, the one that had abducted her, was standing to her left. The third one, old man Tucker, was to her right. They were conversing, but her mind wasn't quite ready to focus on anything they had to say.

"Lord, have mercy. Her baby's gonna come out to-night," Lee Tucker spat a wad of tobacco juice down at his feet.

"How do you know, Daddy?" Tobias looked over the naked girl on the floor. Once again, he found himself jealous of Matty. It wasn't fucking fair that Daddy let *him* have all the fun with these bitches when *he* was the one that had to kidnap them, strip them naked, and lash them up like hogs. Once, just once, he'd like to have his way with them before Matty dropped his inbred seed in them.

"Boy, look between her legs. Her water's broke. Pretty soon her belly's gonna hitch and start pushing that baby outta her. Now, somebody's got to be out here to catch it when it does."

Tobias backed a few steps away. "Oh, no, Daddy. I don't know nuthin' 'bout birthin' no babies!"

Lee Tucker turned and slapped his older son.

"Boy, you don't know nuthin' 'bout nuthin'. You's as dumb as a fucking brainless monkey." Lee rubbed his chin for a moment. "Here's the way things are: Her baby's gonna come out whether we want it to or not. And we just can't keep this baby around. We can't! If anyone comes 'round looking for her and they see we got an infant, they'll know something's up. We got no womenfolk around here, so we sure as hell can't have no babies."

Lee looked down at Betty-June and scowled. "You bitch. You're as big a pain in the ass as my boys. You're complicatin' my life!"

Betty-June whimpered, and her eyes closed up tight

as if she were far away somewhere else.

"Daddy, what's that noise?"

Mathias, who had been standing mute through the whole conversation, was now peering out through the barn window. The moon was high overhead above the fields behind the barn, like a bloody fingernail tearing through the night sky. It illuminated the crops in a ghastly haze. From outside, the noise began to grow, like a concerto of terrified piglets squealing for all their worth.

"For the love of sheep poontang, now what?"

Lee sauntered over to the window and gazed out.

The crop of babies had returned. It was as if for every one they'd cut off the vine, two more had grown back in its place. The ground slithered with wriggly plant-babies under the light of the moon, shrieking their terrible birth wails and pawing blindly into the air for mommies that would never come to claim them. For Lee Tucker, who'd witnessed just about everything under the sun, it was the most god-awful thing he'd ever seen.

He turned to his sons.

"Toby, you's gonna have to stay in here and catch her baby when she delivers it. I gotta take your brother back out in the field. Them crop-babies came back, and it looks like there's a lot of 'em. We gonna have to cut 'em all down and put 'em through the chipper, just like last night. You gotta stay in here and birth her baby. She'll do all the work. All you gotta do is catch it and get rid of it. Bring it right out to me. But don't let her die, ya hear? We's keeping her around to feed your brother!"

Betty-June groaned out loud. She'd been listening

all along, and her response was one of complete resignation, as if she'd come to terms with her fate and was ready to die.

"But Daddy—"

"But nothing! Stay in here and tend to her. And bring the baby to me when it comes out. C'mon, Matty. We got work to do."

Lee Tucker stormed out of the barn with his younger son behind him. When he slammed the door shut behind him, Tobias Tucker began to cry.

Chapter 18

There were so goddamn many of them. It was as if their roots were snaking along far and wide underground, and everywhere they could sprout out through the earth was just about where a new plant-baby could be found. Lee Tucker had only gone three steps into the field when he tromped down on the first plant-baby. It screamed out loud as its plump little body squished under his foot, its tummy collapsing in like a rotten melon and erupting with fetid, bloody organs and entrails. Lee lifted his foot and planted it another step ahead, coming down on *another* plant-baby. Only this time, the sole of his boot came down on its head. The baby head ruptured with a sickening *POP*, and its brains oozed out across the soil in a splash of green-oatmeal gray matter.

Lee stopped and turned toward Mathias, who had frozen still at the edge of the crop.

"Boy, go to the tool shed and get the wheelbarrow and a hoe. We got work to do!"

Mathias lumbered off toward the tool shed.

From all around him, Lee heard the terrible shriek of the plant-babies. They screamed and wailed into the night, their chorus almost deafening the head of the Tucker family. Lee raised his hands and covered his ears and tried to take another step without accidentally trodding on any of the babies. He felt the bump and jostle of tiny arms and legs flailing against him as he moved. Baby fingers tried to grab his boots and pant-legs, but they were too fragile to find any purchase. After a few more paces, he decided to just stop and stand still and wait for Mathias to return with the tools.

The crops were going to have to go. There was no question in his mind. Come sun-up, they were going to have to douse the whole field in gasoline and just set it all alight. He couldn't stand another night of this, another night of horror as the plant-babies birthed themselves. Lee could already feel his chest tightening in terror, the telltale sign of his ticker preparing to give way and send him off into the next world where his sister Loretta would be waiting for him. As the babies screamed around him, he could almost hear her voice calling.

The first pair of arms shot up out of the ground, sending clumps of blood-dampened earth scattering across his boots. And then the first of the dead mommies slowly climbed up out of the soil behind him. She was unclothed, her rotting skin covered from head to toe with foul-smelling earth. Cow shit and soil caked her hair. Her eyes blazed milky-white and angry. There were two huge plates of flappy, scabbed-over skin where her breasts had once been, before Lee's boy Tobias had sliced them off and served them for dinner.

From her vagina, a long, snakelike tendril of umbilical flesh-root sprawled out, linking the corpse to one of the plant-babies somewhere nearby.

Another pair of arms shot up through the soil. Then another. Then, another still. Until the field of vegetables became a graveyard of unearthed revenants.

Lee Tucker tried to scream, but his scream died in his throat as his heart simply burst inside his chest. Reality faded for him as the first of the zombie-moms grabbed him, pulled him close, and bit into his face.

As moonlight faded to darkness, he could see Loretta's face before him. Her lips moved, and he could almost recall the sweet, sweet voice of his sister. It made him think of when they were children and she used to sing along with the choir at church, with a voice so beautiful that it often brought the adults around them to tears.

"Come home, brother...hell is waiting for us."

Mathias was at the edge of the field with the wheelbarrow and hoe when he saw what was happening to his father. Corpses filled the field, all of them naked and missing their breasts. Three or four of them had gathered around Daddy and were slowly ripping him apart and devouring him. He watched as his Daddy's arm was yanked right out of his shoulder socket, stretching out impossibly in long tendrils of stretchy flesh and muscle, until the arm snapped right off the body. All around the ground, plant-babies shrieked and wept as the dead women (most of which he'd fornicated with) ambled about in the moonlight. Several more of them accosted his Daddy before his body just collapsed and fell to the ground. When it did, Matty could see the plant-babies turn and crawl toward his Daddy and begin to feast.

"Daddy! Daddy, are you okay?" It was the only thing he could think of to say.

"What's going on out there?" The voice of Bubba hissed out from beneath the bib of his overalls.

Mathias unbuckled one side and let Bubba peek out.

Bubba gasped in terror. "Run, you idiot! Run!"

Mathias lit off for the barn, not even bothering to let go of the wheelbarrow.

CHAPTER 19

Betty-June slipped in and out of consciousness.

At the moments when the fetus inside her fell still, her mind could slip off into the clouds and fly away, far, far away from her prison inside the barn. When her baby moved, it brought her back down with a jarring severity that made her eyes fly open. She would lift her head and glance about the barn, trying to make a mental inventory of whatever tools and resources she could use to aid in her escape.

Not that she would get very far. Not with her baby ready to slip right out of her womb. If she tried to stand up now, she was certain her baby would tumble out like a toy yo-yo, only it wouldn't spring back upward again.

No, it would simply crash onto the floor, probably killing it upon landing. She would have to deliver it right there. All tied up. And she would be helpless to stop Tobias from hauling it away from her forever.

She glanced up at the Tucker boy, who had fetched a small, wooden milking stool and set his sentry right by her side. Betty-June tried to speak to him, but her voice was gone. All that came out was a whisper.

"Please..." she sobbed. "Please don't let them hurt my baby. You don't have to be like them. Please, please let us go."

"I can't."

The tears were flowing again. She could feel them glide down her skin, leaving cool trails along her heated flesh.

"Please! I'll do anything you want."

"You don't understand," Tobias answered. He looked down at her naked body, still tied fast and sprawled across the floor. Then he turned and spat a greasy wad of tobacco juice onto the floor. "My little brother's got to eat. And my Daddy ain't gonna let you go as long as those titties of yours are producing breast milk. Yer just gonna have to get used to living with us."

Betty-June closed her eyes. She found her mind racing back to all the things she saw as she scanned the barn: The pitchfork and the shovel leaning against the wall to the left of the barn entrance, the workbench against the wall directly across, with the clutter of tools sprawled out across its wooden top. Various lengths of wood in 2x2s and 2x4s, nestled about in odd piles. An old chainsaw with its blade chain fractured and dangling helplessly from the motor mount. An axe, buried nearly to the hilt in one of the support beams, with a rusty, old oil lantern dangling from it.

"My husband will find you," she whispered in a hiss. She opened her eyes and looked up at Toby. "He'll find you, and God help you when he does. He has the law practically in his pocket. He'll find you, and he'll fix you all for what you did to me. I swear to God, Nelson will find you, and he'll make you all suffer."

Tobias sighed and stood up. He stomped past her, and there was the briefest moment when she was sure he was going to go to the workbench and find a tool to cut her loose from the ropes and set her free. Instead, he made his way to the back of the barn where the tractor was parked. There was something directly behind the tractor, something concealed in shadows and bad angles, but it was there nonetheless. It took a moment for it to register in her brain, but when it finally did, she felt her bladder release, and a hot stream of urine flowed out onto the wooden floor beneath her.

Nelson's Mazda.

What the hell is THAT *doing here?*

Tobias grabbed something from inside the tractor's bucket, and with a great amount of grunting and tugging, began to drag something out from around the tired, old machine. When he passed the Ingersoll's giant rear tires, he gave the object one last yank, then let it drop, and Nelson's dead body plunked down on the floor beside her.

She closed her eyes tight, gritted her teeth down hard

together, and began yanking and jerking at the ropes that held her. She could feel the burn of twined fibers against her skin, gouging and snarling as she struggled. Betty-June pulled and pulled until the beam that held her hands began to creak in disapproval. But the knots held.

This is real! she thought. *This is really real. This is how I'm going to die. Like a fucking animal waiting to be slaughtered.*

Betty-June opened her eyes and looked at her dead husband. She could see the stab wounds where something sharp had pierced through his business suit and his blood had spilled out. She could see the panic on his face, how rigor mortis had set in with his eyes still wide and his lips frozen in a wide-open rictus of terror across his clean-shaven skin. She could smell his cologne, and the stink of piss and shit emanating from somewhere inside his silk boxer shorts. Nelson had died badly, painfully, and in that moment, she realized she felt no real love for him whatsoever, nor pride in herself for being his wife.

He died a coward. I can see it on his face. He never even lifted a finger to protect himself.

Tobias plopped back down onto the stool beside her.

"You see?" he said coldly. "Even if I *did* let you go, you have nothing to go home to."

Betty-June's abdomen cramped. It hurt so bad that all the air in her lungs rushed out in one quick breath. It took a few seconds for her to breathe again, and when she did, she looked up at Toby.

"It's coming! My baby is coming."

Chapter 20

Tobias craned his head down so that he was gazing between her legs. The baby's head was just beginning to crown. He was so horrified by the sight that he turned and threw up.

"You have to catch it," Betty-June huffed out in labored whispers. "Please! You have to catch my baby. I can't do it by myself. My hands are tied."

Toby stopped vomiting, wiped his sleeve across his face to dry up the mess and the tears, and shot up to his feet. There was a brief moment when his knees buckled, but he somehow managed to catch himself, forcing the spinning feeling in his brain to ebb and disappear. When it vanished completely, he sprinted over to the workbench, found a hacksaw, and raced back to her side. He began sawing through the ropes. When her hands came loose, Tobias stood up again.

"You're on your own," he said. "Sorry!"

And then he was bolting for the barn door.

It flew open before he could grasp the knob, and then the wood of the door was connecting with his face in one fierce, concussive blast that knocked him right off his feet. Toby dropped to the floor, landed with a hard *thud* as the back of his head collided with the wooden beams, and then he was out like a light.

Mathias flew into the barn, pushing the wheelbarrow through the doorway in crazed desperation. The barrow's wheel caught against his older brother's leg, then flipped upright over the unconscious Tucker boy, crashing down over him like a coffin lid, concealing his body near completely.

"What the hell?" Mathias looked about the barn, not seeing his older brother underneath the overturned wheelbarrow. What he did see was the dead body of the banker dude and the girl that he'd just fornicated with sitting upright beside it.

The naked girl's hands were free; one hand was holding the hacksaw, cutting through the ropes that were lashing her legs to the stall rails. The other hand was stuffed down by her fuck-hole. She turned to face the idiot brute for only a second, and the absolute rage and fear in her eyes actually made Mathias take two steps backward. His body brushed against the doorway, and then his mind was racing back to the horde of dead women outside that had just attacked his Daddy, ripped his limbs off, and devoured him.

"We got to do something! Lady, you have to help me..."

The last of the rope snapped under the snaggle-tooth blade of the saw, and then Betty-June was pushing herself up to her feet. Her hand was still shoved down by her cunny, and Mathias could now see the baby's head sprouting from between her legs. It looked like the world's craziest puppet toy, and Matty thought it reminded him of Bubba. He wondered if it might speak to him the way his conjoined brother did.

Summoning whatever strength she could muster, Betty-June hobbled over to the pitchfork by the wall. She picked up the tool with one hand, and then she was charging right for Mathias, the tines on the tool splayed out before her in one terrible moment of defiance and revenge. She felt the tines passing through the Tucker boy's chest, impaling him right through the bib of his overalls and into the freakish head of his inbred conjoined brother.

She heard Bubba screaming in agony from behind the cloth, wailing and gasping exactly how *she* had as they raped her. Bubba shrieked and wailed as Mathias dropped to his knees, the pitchfork sticking out from his chest like a dinner fork protruding from a Christmas ham. The boy tried to speak, but the only things to pass through his lips were hot, shallow breaths bathed in blood bubbles.

It was the most satisfying thing Betty-June had ever seen.

She dropped quickly to the floor and allowed her body to expel the infant from her womb. When the child came out (it was a boy), she cradled her son in her arms, gently cleaning off the blood and afterbirth with her free hand. With a trembling finger, she swabbed out the babe's mouth and then gave it a quick swat on its rear end. The babe sputtered, then coughed, and then started crying. She swaddled the baby in her arms, gently cuddling it close to her bare skin, and then she slipped out of consciousness.

Chapter 21

She awoke to the sound of something moving outside the barn.

Betty-June sat up, clutching her newborn son close to her bosom. She could hear the sound of movement outside, the sound of feet milling about in the gravel and dirt outside the barn door.

"Help!" she tried to scream, but her vocal cords were still too strained to make any noise. "Somebody help me…" she whispered again.

She heard a groan from underneath the wheelbarrow and knew that the older Tucker boy was coming around. In a few seconds, he would be up again, and he would likely be off to retrieve his Daddy. The body of the younger Tucker boy lay motionless on the floor, the pitchfork still sticking out of his chest. Tobias Tucker would see what she did to his brother, and he would kill her. There was no question in her mind about it. He would kill her, and he would take her baby away and likely kill him, too. Or worse...he would raise it as one of *them!*

The sound was growing louder, as if whoever was milling about outside the barn was now just outside the door.

I have to kill him, she thought. *I have to kill them all if I'm going to get away. I've already killed the big one, and this one is still practically unconscious. If I can get the pitchfork, I can get this one, too. Then I just have to get past their daddy...*

Betty-June glanced over at the body of her dead husband. She was shocked to discover that she still felt no sorrow for him, nor any real trace of love. In the end, she really *wasn't* any different than the Tuckers. There was only life and survival and doing what needed to be done.

She stood up slowly, cradling her infant against her with her left arm. The umbilical cord still dangled from her womb, still connected her with her child. There was a moment when she considered picking the hacksaw up and severing it right then, but she found she liked feeling that connection still there, as if it somehow gave her strength and courage.

You just do what needs to be done, her brain told her, and she was hobbling across the floor to the corpse of Mathias Tucker. With her right hand, she grasped the wooden handle of the pitchfork. With her right foot, she pressed down on the giant's chest, right where the face of Bubba had lived and died, and began to press down, providing resistance. It took a bit of tugging and wiggling, but eventually the tines pulled out of the dead boy's chest cavity, sending four bloody streams behind them as it came free. And then she turned toward the living Tucker boy, who was just beginning to push at the wheelbarrow on top of him.

The first zombie girl walked through the barn door.

It shambled in, her filthy, naked body dropping clumps of soggy, bloody earth onto the floor. The skin of her face had rotted away enough to expose the skull and jawbone beneath. The corpse's jaw quivered up and down in an obscene pantomime of laughter as it looked up and down Betty-June's naked body. And then an almost skeletal arm was pointing at Betty-June's mid-section.

She thought it was pointing at her baby.

"Yes..." she whispered, the tears streaming from her eyes. "They're trying to take away my baby!"

The zombie girl shook her head slowly, as if to say, "No." Instead, it pointed toward her breasts and then moved its bony arm to the empty hollows where its own breasts had been. The zombie girl cocked her head to the side, its face stretched into a frown of bone and grizzle. Its jaw moved slowly, mouthing only one word:

"Boobies!"

And then more zombie girls were flooding into the barn. They moved slowly, pained by death and decay, leaving a trail of filth as they stumbled through the door All of them entered; nearly two dozen women who had been abducted, raped, murdered, and had their breasts removed and consumed by the Tucker family. They filed in quietly and formed a semicircle around Betty-June and her newborn son as if they were the new Madonna and Christ. Betty-June wept warm, bitter tears for them.

The wheelbarrow toppled over without warning, and Tobias Tucker sat up, rubbing his head. He turned and looked at the dead women, this sisterhood-of-the-soil, and let out a scream. The dead girls all turned as one, and then they converged upon him before he could make it to his feet. Dead jaws opened wide and began to consume. Tobias Tucker was alive and very much awake as they began to feast.

The zombie girl (the one who first came in) raised a dead hand and pointed toward the barn door. Betty-June nodded and then made her exodus into the moon-lit night, her babe still tucked against her naked body.

She could still hear the weeping of the plant-babies in the crops behind her as she fled from the Tucker farm for good.

Epilogue

Getting out alive had been like winning the lottery.

Being rescued at the side of the road by a Good Samaritan in an 18-wheeler (who blew off his haul route and brought her and her baby directly to the Cold Currant Medical Center instead) was like having the cosmos realigning itself for her convenience.

Having the insurance company issue her a check to cover the claim on Nelson's life insurance policy was a bona fide miracle. Betty-June Gray was now *the* richest woman in Cold Currant (and if the girls at the café didn't have dirt on her before, they sure did *now!*).

She told the police everything, including how she'd murdered at least one of the Tucker boys to escape. They hadn't believed a word she'd said, but a quick trip

out to the Tucker farm provided all the proof they needed. Eventually, the State Police were brought in, and when
they couldn't figure out the whole mess, they called in
the F.B.I. The results were all the same: the case was
too fantastic to ever decipher the truth, so they fudged
facts until they could provide a more palatable explana-
tion. In the end, no charges were ever brought against
Betty-June Gray.

Betty-June and Jesus Gray (she'd struggled to find a
name for her only son and finally picked the only name
she could associate with any *real* miracles) moved upstate
before the year was over. She found a nice piece of
land up north, with a house that wasn't too big or pride-
ful for her to spend her remaining days on the planet.
There was enough land for Jesus to play and grow and
have a life completely free of the madness she'd escaped
from at the hands of the Tucker Blood Cult (the name
the media had picked for them, not what *she* would have
called them).

On hot summer nights, Betty-June found herself
at the hands of insomnia, and when she did sleep, images
of the Tucker boys and their Daddy and the dead women
who had allowed her to pass unharmed, as if she were
already one of them, filled her dreams. When the river
ran high, she could almost hear the wail of the plant-
babies, crying along with the churning water.

Jesus, thankfully, remembered nothing.

It brought her great comfort to watch him play out
in the backyard. He grew quickly, at an almost alarming
rate, and there were times when she could see traces

of the late Nelson Gray in his face and in his posture. And he was always happy, which made *her* happy. When the sun set over the western horizon of the river, casting long, tall shadows from the smokestacks of the Atkins Chemical Company across their backyard, Betty-June and Jesus would creep down to the riverbanks and watch for the evening stars to appear. They always made a wish on the first star and never told each other what they wished for.

Secretly, Betty-June simply wished to forget.

ABOUT THE AUTHOR

Peter N. Dudar was born in Albany, New York. A graduate of Christian Brothers Academy and an alumnus of the University at Albany, Dudar now resides in Lisbon Falls, Maine, where he works fulltime for the United States Postal Service. He is a proud member of the New England Horror Writers, the Horror Writers of Maine, and is a founding member of the Tuesday Mayhem Society; a local writers group. He lives with his wife Amy, their two daughters, and a dog named Princess Cupcake Zippity Dudar. He insists he had nothing to do with naming the dog.

Betty-June Gray's adventures continue in:

The Mississippi Glory Hole Mutilations

PROLOGUE

On the morning of July 17th, 2013, Lee Tucker and his two sons, Tobias and Mathias, were visited by a representative of the Cold Currant Savings and Loan to present foreclosure documents for the farm their family had owned and operated for generations. The representative, Bank Vice President Willie Nelson Gray, was murdered in cold blood. His young bride, Betty-June Gray, was later abducted by Tobias Tucker and brought as an offering to the deformed, conjoined twin of his younger brother Mathias. Kidnapped and sexually assaulted, Betty-June Gray escaped from what the annals of American crime labeled "The Blood Cult of the Booby Farmers."

At the time, young Betty-June was pregnant and days

away from delivering the child her late husband would never get to meet. In his absence, she was forced to abandon the life of luxury his insurance policy had provided and return to her roots as a young, under-educated woman in the deep south, where she struggled to raise her child, Jesus, who'd obviously been adversely affected by the toxic waste of the Atkins Chemical Plant, up north from their home on the Mississippi River.

The following is based on a true story.

On a hot summer night in Mississippi...

The Headhunter sat at the far end of the lounge, watching quietly as the state's junior representative entered the Flesh Fantastique, swished past Dallas, the doorman, and tried to cop a feel of another patron's ass on his way over to the bar. The woman looked moderately annoyed at first, and when she saw the dude with the cheap suit and the big, sweaty forehead, she recognized Matt Wentz as that sleazy politician who was just exposed on national news for sex-trafficking a minor after his latest political fundraiser. The proprietor of the Flesh Fantastique, a tall, burly fellow named Manlius Latham, also noticed. The Flesh Fantastique wasn't a whore-house, not like the Bunny Ranch out in Nevada or some of those other houses of ill repute in New York or Los Angeles; it was a hedonism club. The building was a two-story townhouse in the upper east end of the city; built in the early twentieth century, it had served as a speakeasy in the 20s, an orphanage in the 40s, and later fell into the hands of Latham's family in the 70s during the city's restoration era. The bald man with the gold earring and the perfectly trimmed beard had turned the upper floor into a palace of fantasy suites and bedrooms and the basement into a dungeon labyrinth of bondage and discipline cells. The first floor was a mixture of cocktail lounge and island oasis of sofas with soft, poofy pillows and silk tapestries. Many of these sofas were filled with couples and ménages à trois who openly drank and cavorted lasciviously as Wentz passed by. Latham's job was to make sure that the patrons followed the club's rules so that no laws were broken so there was no chance of inviting in undercover police officers and giving them cause to shut him down. By the look on his face, he was already planning to remove the gentleman with the broad, sweaty forehead.

The Headhunter watched as Latham made his way past both the clothed and unclothed patrons and confronted the junior representative before he could order a drink and seek out a consensual lay.

Latham spoke quietly, but that didn't matter. The Headhunter could practically read his lips.

"I can't have you in here, Mathew. Not while you're being investigated for your...uh...indiscretion."

"Bullshit, you can't," Wentz retorted, his wide, bloodshot eyes practically molesting the topless woman who passed him on her way to the bar. "We both know I have enough leverage in the State House to have this place closed down. Your little club here was grandfathered into law and gets away with a lot of technicalities, but we both know the *moral fiber* of our great state's Bible Belt would fill this whole city with protestors if they knew what was going on here. Now, if you'll excuse me, I need to find myself a nice ass to fuck so I can get back home to the wife and children."

Wentz was speaking loud enough for the whole room to hear. The Headhunter watched silently, feeling that tingle of inner rage coming to a boil inside. This creep was most definitely the right target. The *next* target.

"Look around this place," Latham said, maintaining his cool. The proprietor was actually smiling. "My clientele *know* who you are. I can assure you, Mister Wentz, you're not going to find a patron here, female or male, that wants to be associated with a pedophile." Latham nodded toward Dallas, who'd been watching all along and had his hand conspicuously dipped inside his blue blazer, his fingers resting on the strap of a concealed holster. Wentz's face blanched, and new beads of sweat formed on his huge forehead, some trickling down his face and onto his jacket. The Headhunter noticed the American flag pin on his lapel and the way his red necktie made his face look like a turkey with an enormously long wattle.

"I don't want no trouble," the junior representative said, and the growing panic in his eyes was abundantly evident. The Headhunter smiled. This was all going so smoothly. It felt like being a spider and watching that plump, obnoxious fly getting ready to land right inside its web. "…and I'm *not* a pedophile! The age of consent is seventeen here in Mississippi, and that bitch was happy to take my money and come party with me. If you saw her, you'd have done the *same thing*."

"No, I really *wouldn't*," Latham replied. He nodded again, and now Dallas was on his way across the room, his hand still inside his blazer, still resting on the butt of his Glock. Dallas was an older gentleman, with dark hair and crow's feet around the eyes, and comported himself with such a suave sense of dignity that the female patrons of the club often made passes at him, not even realizing he was working.

"You're making a mistake," Wentz protested. "Senator McDonnell is gonna retire someday, and *I'll* be the one who takes his place in D.C.!"

"Dallas, escort this gentleman to his car, please. And don't make a scene. People have their smartphones out and are recording us with their cameras." Latham turned back to Wentz. "Mister Wentz, unless you want this little interaction going viral on social media, leave quietly and don't return until your legal troubles have been remedied. Do I make myself clear?"

Dallas smiled, put his free hand on Wentz's shoulder, and directed him toward the door. "Let's go, Mister Wentz."

"Did you hear me? I'm gonna be a senator someday, and I *will* shut your little fucking sex club down! I paid a *lot* of fucking money to become a member here, and dammit, I ain't leaving until I get my rocks off. You got that?"

The Headhunter already knew what was going to happen next. Could see it a mile away. The first floor of the building had a row of closets over beyond the bar. During the prohibition era, the doors actually had false façades attached to hide their existence, allowing bartenders to hide kegs of beer, jars of whiskey, and bottles of bathtub gin in the event of a raid. Now, they looked more like a row of booths in an adult video store, where dudes pumped singles into an automated cash machine and jerked off as the video screen played their favorite selection of porn. Surely, these closets had similar offerings, but in a club like this, it offered just a little bit more…

With any luck, the room behind the closets was empty. That was the whole enticement; someone would be waiting behind the wall. For some, the kink was to be able to enjoy the thrill of pleasuring someone without ever seeing their face. And that was exactly what Latham was explaining to Wentz now. Wentz's eye went wide with glee as the bald gentleman with the gold earring whispered and nodded toward the doors.

The Headhunter rose quietly, patted the purloined steak knife concealed discretely inside her pantyhose, and made her way toward a door behind the bar. The door was unlocked. The room was empty. She pulled a compact out of her purse, checked her lipstick, and waited for the junior representative to push his erection through the hole in the closet wall.

Chapter 1

Betty-June Gray considered herself a fast learner, despite her mama always insisting she would be better off just finding a man to do all her heavy thinking for her. And goddamn it, she'd *had* a man once upon a time—not a great man by any stretch, but Nelson Gray had done right by her until those inbred assholes on the Tucker farm murdered him. Now, here she was on her second day of waitressing at the Pig-Whistle Truck Stop Diner and noticing that uptight bitch, Catie, was stealing one of her booths over by the jukebox. With the diner's other waitress, Frida, off for the night, it was just the two of them hustling tables, and Betty-June had already decided she hated Catie. The box was currently playing that song by Merle Haggard about being twenty-one in prison, and Catie was chawing and snapping her bubblegum like a cow, occasionally blowing messy pink bubbles and then licking the sticky wad off her lips with her tongue as she slurped it back into her mouth. Betty-June wiped her hands off on her apron, then clutched her sweaty fists against her hips.

"What can I do for ya?" Catie asked, snapping the gum noisily, and Betty-June noticed that at some point Catie had to have ducked into the lady's room to apply fresh lipstick. The woman had to be in her fifties, her long, straight hair—once platinum but now a vaporous white that seemed to reflect red from the neon sign over the bar—pulled into a tight bun. Catie glanced up at her, their eyes meeting, and then that obnoxious bitch actually smiled at her.

The trucker, a tubby fellow in a stained t-shirt displaying Larry the Cable Guy, flashed a grin of stained, crooked teeth. His cheeks flushed crimson, and his eyes lowered toward the table as he spoke. His right hand dipped below the table, presumably to fish through his pocket for something. When his hand returned to the table, it was filled with crumpled dollar bills, which he pushed toward the waitress.

"I'd like an order of double-cherry pie," he said, removing his hand from the wad of money and placing it back down in his lap.

Catie blew a bubble, allowing the gum to snap across her freshly applied lipstick, and then lasciviously lassoed it back inside her mouth with her tongue. She reached across the table, picked up the money, glanced down to see how much was there, and then stuffed the cash inside the pocket of her apron. Catie leaned down, whispered something into the dude's ear, and then took off for the kitchen area. The trucker sat there for about a minute, his beady eyes nervously scanning the restaurant to see if anyone was watching. Betty-June turned away quickly, pretending to run her washcloth over a nearby table, trying to hide her surveillance. A few more seconds passed, and then the dude got up from his table— making sure he'd left nothing behind—and waddled hurriedly into the men's room.

Betty-June noticed these things and immediately dropped the cloth on the table. She flew through the kitchen, quietly passing Luis and Pami (the two Latino cooks) looking for Catie. She could smell the grease from meat and bacon frying on the grill and the odor of the garbage cans that she already knew she'd get stuck emptying before her shift was over. Bluebottle flies buzzed around the overhead lights, their buggy bodies bumping against the long halogen tubes, and then divebombing the garbage cans for a brief rest and a bite to eat.

This place is a fucking shithole! she thought to herself, peeking first into the walk-in refrigerator, and then around the grill to the custodial area, where the mop and bucket sat idly inside the mop sink.

Nobody.

Betty-June was about to turn around and head back into the dining area when she heard a soft moaning. It seemed to be coming from the supply closet beyond the custodial area. Following the layout of the building, that room would diametrically fall behind the far side of...

The men's room.

Betty-June stood on one foot and removed her white high-heeled shoe, and then switched feet to remove the other, and then she tiptoed past the mop sink toward the supply closet. She reached out a trembling hand, turned the doorknob so slowly and quietly, and then giggled out loud when she saw Catie Walsh down on her knees.

There was a hole in the far wall, presumably adjoined to the farthest stall in the men's room, and Catie's head was bobbing back and forth in front of it. When Catie heard the intruder, she stopped what she was doing and spun around, exposing the far-from-impressive white penis protruding through the hole in the plasterboard. The trucker dude's cock was rock hard and poking through like a baby water moccasin. There was an audible gasp from the other side of the wall, followed by a timid voice asking, "Hello? Everything okay back there?"

"Hey, get the fuck out of here!" Catie hollered, and Betty-June suddenly noticed the wad of bubblegum dangling precariously just beside the hole in the wall. It occurred to her that she'd only been in this room maybe two or three times on her first night of work, and she hadn't even noticed it. Betty-June covered her mouth just as the guffaw burst through, and then she was yanking the door shut behind her as Catie wrapped her lips around the trucker's penis to finish what she'd started.

Earl, the bartender, had already switched the television from ESPN to Cable World News by the time Betty-June returned to the dining room. The anchorman was currently rehashing the latest about the Headhunter, and how Mississippi's junior representative had been castrated by this mysterious sexual predator/vigilante. *Good! I hope this Headhunter chops the cock off every last rapist in the whole state!* She picked up her abandoned washcloth and went to wipe down another table when she noticed a new trucker had taken the same booth as the dude who Catie was currently servicing. The guy was wearing a hunter green t-shirt and a John Deere cap

Oh, Christ, the same hat that Tobias Tucker was wearing when he...

She froze in her tracks, gripping her order pad and pen in a death clutch. She could still recall the greasy face of the man who had abducted her seven years ago, and that of his rapist brother, Mathias. Betty-June had tried so hard to suppress those memories and deal with the agonizing trauma that spilled back into her life in all those unwanted moments when she was trying to regain her own identity and be a mother to Jesus Gray.

If this man orders a double-cherry pie, it means he wants me to go into the back room so he can stick his penis through that hole in the wall and put it in my mouth.

The thought was broken when the dude in the Larry the Cable Guy t-shirt burst through the men's room door, simultaneously pulling up the fly of his Wrangler dungarees and keeping his face directly on the Pig-Whistle Diner's exit door. The guy flew past Betty-

June, and she could smell the cheap cologne and the flop sweat undoubtedly dribbling from his armpits and on down his rotund belly. She watched him through the plate glass windows as the dude yanked open the door to his rig and stuffed that enormous gut up behind the steering wheel.

"Betty-June, wake up," Earl shouted from behind the bar. "That guy's waiting to order."

She wondered if Earl knew about the glory hole. Of *course,* he had to. Men ruled everything. Earl wasn't quite as old as Catie, but the guy must have worked at the Pig-Whistle Diner for years, and you don't spend years turning a blind eye to stuff like waitresses whoring themselves out for extra cash under the table, or at least giving blowjobs in the supply closet. Betty-June felt as if her life was flashing before her eyes with every step she took toward the far booth, thinking about her dead husband—and how the Tucker boys had murdered him in cold blood seven years ago—and about their only son, Jesus Gray, back at home in their ranch-style house less than a mile away from the interstate. She could feel the butterflies of dread fluttering in the pit of her belly and the goose pimples breaking out along her arms and neck, and the feeling of shame she'd felt as that trucker rescued her and delivered her directly to the Cold Currant Medical Center on that awful night all those years ago.

If he orders a double-cherry pie, I'll grab the utensils off the table and jamb the fork as hard as I can into his eye socket and—

"Good evening, ma'am," the trucker said, removing his John Deere hat and placing it on the table. "Think you can rustle me up a cup of coffee and a breakfast burrito?"

"What?"

The trucker grinned politely, his warm blue eyes gazing into hers. "You're new here, ain't ya?"

Betty-June glanced nervously toward the bar to see if Earl was watching them. On the television above the bar, the news network was now showing an interview with Senator Rich McDonnell, who was blustering the same old horse shit about the Atkins Chemical Company *not* being guilty of polluting the Mississippi River watershed. Everyone in Mississippi knew that creep was taking kickbacks from the lobbyists who represented Atkins. Deep down, everyone was a whore. It was just that some bluster rather than swallow.

Oh, you lying sack of...

Earl was nowhere to be seen, but Catie was sauntering back onto the dining room floor. That nasty bitch had obviously fixed her lipstick *again* after sucking off that last trucker. What did the comedian always say as his catchphrase? "Get 'er done?" Catie once again made eye contact with Betty-June, and then she was moving toward the booth, still chomping noisily on her gum and smiling like the cat that ate the canary.

"Oh, hi, Roy!" she said, blowing a great big bubble with her gum and then making a show of slurping it back into her mouth with her long, pink tongue. Watching her almost made Betty-June gag.

"Hey, Catie," the trucker replied. "I was just—"

"This is *my* booth, honey," Betty-June mewled. "You just run along now. And be sure to wipe off that blob of stuff dripping down your tits."

Catie's cheeks burned red as she looked down at her bosom and noticed the giant glob of semen running down her blouse. She turned and stormed off back into the kitchen, nearly running into Earl, who was returning from the walk-in refrigerator with two more cases of Budweiser for the bar. Betty-June returned her attention to the young trucker, who was obviously only there to grab a bite before hitting the interstate for whatever destination lie in his future.

Chapter 2

At seven years old, Jesus Gray stood nearly six feet tall and showed no sign of his growth slowing down. Mama would tell him it was because he always drank his milk and ate all his veggies at dinnertime, but the boy wasn't stupid. He would be starting second grade come the fall, and although the other kids he knew from kindergarten and first grade weren't openly cruel about it, they would be soon enough. Jesus knew there was something different about himself, and it hovered uncomfortably over that line of anxiety that seemed to fester whenever he tried to ask mama about why his daddy didn't live with them or why she never talked about him other than to tell him that Nelson Gray loved him with all his heart and soul.

But not enough to stick around and be his daddy.

He thought about these things as the green LED

numbers of his digital clock flashed 11:17 p.m., and Aunt Laverne sat in the living room drinking her beer and watching *PERPS* reruns until mama came home from work at midnight. Once upon a time, mama had had enough money to stay at home all day with him, and she'd been his bestest friend in the whole wide world—even better than Danny Martin had once been before he got caught trying to steal Jesus's Devil Dogs from his *Iron Man* lunchbox. Aunt Laverne never even pretended to be his friend. She offered to babysit so that mama could return to work on the conditions that Betty-June kept the cable connected and stocked the fridge with beer. And the moment mama left for work earlier in the evening, Aunt Laverne plopped her fat ass down on the sofa and cracked open her first Rolling Rock. When it came time for dinner, Aunt Laverne helped herself to the leftovers in the fridge and hollered at him to come on out and fix a bowl of cereal if he meant to eat something before bed. Jesus skipped the cereal and fixed a paper plate with Saltine crackers and shredded bits of baloney and Kraft cheese singles instead. He wolfed them down in silence, staring out his bedroom window at the streetlamp in front of their house, where a hundred moths fluttered around the halogen bulb, casting strange but comforting shadows over his bedroom wall.

There was something beautiful about the moths. Almost hypnotizing. After "lights out," they were his nocturnal companions until his eyelids grew heavy enough to fall asleep. The night before, on Mama's first night at work, Jesus had fallen asleep watching them flit and flap about, but tonight he really, *really* wanted to stay awake just long enough to hear Aunt Laverne's car roar into life and drive away, and for him to be able to kiss his mother goodnight before sleep overcame him.

But it felt so hard. The late summer crickets were already screeching their bedtime chorus, and the moths were flitting about so merrily around the lamppost. He could see their wings flapping as they eclipsed the lamp-light. Even at seven years old, Jesus found himself wondering how wonderful it must be to just fly away from all the bad things in life, to fly wherever he pleased without a care in the world, without worrying if Aunt Laverne was going to suddenly throw the door open to check in on him before going back to her beer and her television shows where white men with copper badges beat and handcuffed young black men for her amusement. God, he missed mommy and hated that it wasn't just him and her anymore.

That little freak has *to be asleep by now!*

Laverne Mason picked up her fifth Rolling Rock, chugged it down, then set the empty bottle next to the others on the plastic tray-table with the Confederate flag stenciled on its surface. She was buzzed, and that was good. Not too drunk to risk driving home once her niece got home from work and getting pulled over by one of the staties out on the freeway, but comfortable enough to tolerate babysitting her monstrous seven-year-old nephew, who now dwarfed her anytime the two were in proximity. The Mason family had never been guilty of being too tall; her daddy barely stood at 5'8", and none of his progeny ever eclipsed that height. Laverne barely made it to 5'5", and that was in the high heels she wore to the Currant County Baptist Church on Sundays. She never said it out loud, but Jesus Gray scared the shit out of her. He was unnatural, and that only happened when Satan's finger touched a person's life. *And he's only seven! That means he ain't done growing yet!* Laverne threw a cautious glance over toward the door to the boy's bedroom and then turned away in a hurry. Maybe another Rolling Rock would give her the guts to get up and go check on him.

On the television, the officer on *PERPS* was on foot, chasing down another African-American perpetrator somewhere in New Orleans, claiming to only want to question the guy, but his taser was already drawn and waiting for a clear shot to subdue that perpetrating son-of-a-bitch with a high-voltage dose of the law. Behind him, his partner had a baton drawn and ready to "convince the thug to comply." Laverne picked up the last bottle of Rolling Rock, twisted off the cap, and took a huge swig as she waited to see if the darkie would get the beating he so desperately had coming.

And then, without warning, she heard the window in Jesus's room being thrown wide open. Laverne set the bottle down, stood up, and stared at the bedroom door, her heart rate creeping up into the panic area her doctor insisted wasn't safe for her blood pressure to go. When the front door of the ranch house flew open behind her, Laverne Mason screamed out loud and nearly peed in her panties.

"Aunt Laverne, what's going on?" Betty-June pulled her key out of the doorknob and closed the front door behind her.

"Oh, holy shit, child! You scared the hell out of me!" Laverne panted. "Jesus must have woken up from a bad dream or something. I thought I heard him opening his bedroom window."

Betty-June dropped her tote bag by the table in the foyer and stepped into the living room. She noticed Aunt Laverne's pile of empty beer bottles but dismissed them immediately. Rolling Rock was still pretty cheap, and if she'd had to pay a real babysitter, it would have cost her a lot more than that. And based on her tips for the evening, she actually made out okay for her shift, even with the discovery she'd made about double-cherry pies at the Pig-Whistle truck stop. If all went well, she would make out just fine and never have to fill *that* particular order. There had been a steady stream of truckers who merely wanted a decent meal and enough caffeine to make it to either Jackson or the outer destinations on their manifest without their testosterone kicking in and requesting a blow job. Maybe men weren't such pigs after all. It hurt her heart to realize that her late husband Nelson hadn't been a pig, but a sweet—if not nerdy—guy to be married to. When Jesus was older, she would explain that very sentiment.

"Did you check on him?"

"No!" Aunt Laverne grabbed her half-finished bottle of beer and scarfed it down. "That boy... He ain't natural, child. I ain't never seen no seven-year-old as tall as he is. I'm telling you, baby, he's the Devil's work!"

"No, he *ain't*!" Betty-June marched right past her, ignoring the television and heading straight for her son's bedroom door. "And you just be mindful about what you say in my house! You hear me, Aunt Laverne? My son is *not* a freak! He's a good boy, and if he's bigger than usual, it's because of that Atkins chemical plant. Believe me; I've seen the horror they've caused."

Betty-June grasped the doorknob, twisted hard, and threw her son's bedroom door open. When she saw inside, she gasped in terror.

The bedroom light was on, and with his window wide open, the moths had flown inside his room. Dozens of them, flitting about the overhead light, bumping and bouncing off the ceiling tiles and the glass light globe, and against themselves. And sitting upon his bed, his legs folded crisscross apple sauce, Jesus Gray sat with his eyes rolled back into their sockets and his mouth wide open, trying to catch the moths inside his gaping maw as if he'd meant to swallow them. When he noticed her in the doorway, his cheeks flushed, and tears streamed down his face.

"Hi, mom. Look at all the friends I have now!"

The moths flitted and fumbled against the overhead light and the tiles of the drop ceiling. They flew around the room, darting about the boy and around Betty-June as she stared slack-jawed at her son. Aunt Laverne was shouting from the living room, casting out prayers and Christian admonishments as she waddled toward the bedroom, but Betty-June was seconds faster. She slammed the door shut before the intruders could flutter off into her living room, and then she was racing over to Jesus and wrapping her arms around him. She pulled him into a tight embrace, pushing his face against her shoulder and running her fingers through the boy's long, brown hair. *Nelson's hair. The same hair that Nelson's granddaddy had. My son has my eyes, but he has Nelson's face and hair.* She held him tight and shivered every time a moth flapped against her cheeks and forearms.

"Oh, honey, why did you do this? Bugs are *not* your friends, sweetie. You can't just open your window up and invite them in. How am I going to get them all out of your room so you can go to sleep?"

But her boy was already asleep. He'd drifted off into slumber the moment she put her arms around him. Betty-June lay her son down in his bed and pulled his *MARVEL* superheroes blanket up around him, making sure that his legs were curled up just enough on the twin-sized bed so that his feet didn't hang uncovered off the edge. When she was convinced that he was safe and resting comfortably, she went about the task of closing the window and swatting every last moth with a rolled-up copy of the *Currant County Register*. By the time she was finished, Aunt Laverne was long gone. All that remained were six empty beer bottles and the sound of another unnecessarily violent arrest by a band of good-ol' boys who couldn't care less if black lives mattered.

In the penthouse suite of the *Artemis Hotel* in Jackson, Senator McDonnell sat in the jacuzzi and scrolled through the dozens of voicemail messages on his cellphone. The hooker beside him stroked his drug-induced erection beneath the rolling bubbles, her long, flowing cotton candy-pink hair brushing against her nipples. McDonnell had no idea what the woman's name was— or if she was even of legal age—but that didn't matter. It *wasn't* Muriel, that gold-digging mail-order bride of his, who had only married him for his wealth and for immigration status, and that was just fine. Muriel was half his age—*no,* less *than half his age*—and they both knew the senator would not live forever and that she would eventually inherit his millions. Muriel knew about the hookers. *He* knew about Muriel Yao's happily-ever-after once he was dead, and both of them seemed to be okay with the arrangement, so McDonnell closed his eyes and enjoyed the hooker's hand rubbing and squeezing his crank.

"Oh, you like that, huh?" the young woman purred

coyly, watching as the old man closed his eyes and moaned in reply. McDonnell lifted the cellphone away from the water, being extremely cautious to *not* drop the device into the bubbling jets of the jacuzzi. That cellphone was his whole life at this point; his contacts, emails, and messages aided and abetted in controlling a multi-million-dollar empire both within the capacity of his elected status and with every last shady compromise beneath the table. The fact was, he would *eat* that fucking phone piece by piece before the law or the lamestream media ever got their hands on it. In the suite room, the television was playing Cable World News, and McDonnell could hear the voice of their anchorman, Truth Carson, releasing a late-breaking news report.

"Protestors have now gathered around the Atkins Chemical Plant in Currant County, Mississippi, demanding America's pioneer producer of industrial cleaning supplies halt their waste disposal policies immediately. Democratic officials are demanding the Environmental Protection Agency survey the damage they believe has been caused to the Mississippi River watershed due to complaints filed across the state. Atkins has been investigated in the past over issues of possible toxicity, but the chemical company has always complied, and with the assurance and support of Senator Rich McDonnell..."

"Holy shit, they're talking about *you!*" the hooker exclaimed, suddenly letting go of McDonnell's penis and turning over to mount him right there inside the hot tub. McDonnell's eyes were still closed, still enjoying her services, but his ears were hyper-alert and tuned in to the breaking news report, and as his Viagra-induced boner slid inside the girl's hot, tight pussy, McDonnell heard the anchorman saying that "the senator could not be reached for comment." His eyes opened, and he swung his cellphone between his face and the young hooker's tits.

He saw the text message immediately, still unread and unanswered. He clicked "open" and read the message.

"You *need* to get your ass to Cold Currant and DEAL WITH THIS! The fucking libtards are EVERYWHERE, and they will shut us down if you don't intervene IMMEDIATELY!"

Followed by a half-dozen phone calls from both Cable World News and the local Mississippi affiliates, who were also hyper-aware of what was going down as this unnamed hooker was riding the cock that should have been the sole property of Muriel Yao.

McDonnell sighed.

"Honey, what's your name?"

The hooker was bouncing up and down in his lap, her tight pussy enveloping his short but medicinally rigid wang with a ferocity he would have never been able to match, even in his prime.

"Oh! Oh god, give it to me! Give it to me, you fucking stallion!"

Senator McDonnell gave it to her, closing his eyes and shooting his works as deep as he could inside her. He hoped the chlorinated water of the jacuzzi would be enough to sterilize whatever live sperm he could still create before it could impregnate her. Miss No-Name-Hooker would have him over a barrel if she reported that she was carrying his child, and McDonnell found himself already wondering if he would need to contact Louie the Fixer to make another problem go away.

"What's your name," he repeated.

The girl gathered up handfuls of suds from the water's surface and splashed them across her bare tits until he could no longer see her nipples.

"I'm Champagne," she giggled, pinching her nipples playfully as his spent erection wiggled out of her vagina. "Just like the bubbly water we're sitting in."

"Your real name," McDonnell said, lifting the girl off his lap. Champagne slipped a hand down beneath the surface to try and grasp his cock again. McDonell shot his arm down through the hot, bubbly water and grabbed the girl's wrist, twisting it above the water.

"Ouch! Hey, you're not supposed to hurt me."

"You're name!"

"Traci! Traci Rivers," the girl said, fear now stretching across her face where the phony coital elation had been moments before. "And if you hurt me, I'll tell the whole fucking world."

McDonnell's grip loosened, and she pulled her arm away. "I have no intention of hurting you. I only wanted to know who I was fucking. And you should know who you're fucking *with*. I have people *everywhere*, Traci Rivers. And if you ever go shooting your mouth off about me, I can assure you my people will come for *you*. In fact, I'll have people waiting down in the lobby to follow you home, so I'll know *exactly* where you live. Are we clear?"

The hooker lifted herself out of the jacuzzi and threw a robe around her naked body.

"We're clear," she whispered. McDonnell could see the girl was trembling, and he was almost certain she was a year or two shy of eighteen.

"Good. There's five hundred dollars in cash on my dresser. You take it and get the fuck out of here. If I want your services again, I'll have people come for you. And you'd better not turn me down if you take my meaning."

Champagne was trembling harder now, and tears formed in the corners of her eyes. Beads of water from the hot tub covered her bare skin where the robe didn't, and his spunk oozed from her cooch to run down her leg. Like the other hookers before her, she now belonged to him. Traci—a.k.a. Champagne—nodded quietly, turned, and fled the bathroom. He could hear her sobbing as she threw her clothes on and slammed the door behind her.

Senator McDonnell lifted his cellphone, scrolled through the missed calls until he found the number he wanted, then dialed.

When his connection answered, he whispered, "This is Senator Rich McDonnell. I'll be in Cold Currant by Wednesday to handle the situation. You boys really fucked things up, and I'm a-gonna have to rescue your asses once again. And it will cost you big! For the time being, do *not* make any public statements, do *not* hold any press conferences, and for the love of *God*, do not allow Cable World News to discover any critical information or intimidate you into any form of press conference. Truth

Carson can suck my dick! He better not hear a fucking peep from our camp until I get this shit straightened out. Am I clear? Y'all don't do a fucking thing until I get there to straighten things out!"

McDonnell pressed the "end call" icon on his cellphone and closed his eyes. By his own estimation, Truth Carson was the fucking Devil, himself, and the last thing he needed was to have Cable World News exposing the nefarious activities of the Atkins Chemical Corporation for the damage it had already done, or the undisclosed dealings it had with the Mississippi senator to protect it.

Jesus Gray was sound asleep in his bed when his mother cleaned the last greasy stain of dead moths off his bedroom wall. She'd scoured most of the bedroom with Atkins Disinfectant Wipes after collecting all the dead moths in her child's bedroom trashcan. Betty-June had lost count at some point after the first four or five dozen, and the wadded-up sterilizing wipes covered their squished, lifeless bodies like a death shroud. For this much she was glad because if she had to look inside the plastic *Piggly Wiggly* shopping bag lining the pail, she would probably have thrown up that nasty hamburger and French fries Earl gave her back at the end of her shift. Earl was a good shit. He had recognized her name from all the newspaper articles after Betty-June had escaped from the Tucker farm. Earl brought the subject up on her first night at work, and he had told her flat out that if she was uncomfortable talking about it, he would keep his trap shut until she trusted him enough. She could have kissed him right then and there for that kindness, but the reality was that he *knew*. And if his word was good, if he could manage to *not* spill the beans to Catie, then maybe she would eventually trust him. God knew, she needed somebody, *anybody*, to just listen.

Aunt Laverne was all she really had at the moment, and all Aunt Laverne cared about was herself. Betty-June already regretted making this arrangement, but short of quitting and trying to find a decent day job while her boy was in school seemed like an impossibility. Life in a small town meant secrets and harbored resentments, and after Nelson died—

After Nelson was murdered!

—Betty-June could not bear the thought of working side-by-side with the girls she grew up with knowing that at one point she was the richest woman in Currant County and was now flat broke again.

It felt like her miseries never ended.

After she finished tidying up the mess, Jesus Gray's mother bent down, kissed her sleeping son on his forehead, and then snatched up the plastic bag from the garbage pail and pulled his bedroom door closed behind her.

Country life not to your liking? Then why not
check out the Big City life and join the parade...

The Goat Parade

PETER N. DUDAR

The **GOAT**
PARADE

"A darkly absorbing journey into
evil with a decidedly human heart
beating at its core..."
–Ed Kurtz, author of *The Rib From Which I Remake the World*
and *At the Mercy of Beasts*

"...frightening, and a whole hell of
a lot of fun to read...horror the
way it is supposed to be written."
–Tony Tremblay, author of *The Seeds of Nightmares*
and *The Moore House*

www.ingramcontent.com/pod-product-compliance
Lightning Source LLC
Chambersburg PA
CBHW060746210726

48292CB00015B/2805